ESCAPE FROM HELL

ESCAPE FROM HELL

Brian O'Donnell

National Library of Australia Cataloguing-in-Publication

Creator: O'Donnell, Brian, author.

Title: Escape from hell / Brian O'Donnell.

ISBN: 9780648014645 (paperback)
         9780648014652 (ebook)

Subjects: Teenage boys-Fiction.
          Cooking-Fiction.
          Romance fiction.

Cover and Typeset: Pickawoowoo Publishing Group

Printed & channel distribution:

Lightning Source | Ingram (USA/UK/EUROPE/AUS)

Table of Contents

PREFACE

ESCAPE FROM HELL

Escape from hell is the story of a teenage boy's escape from his mean, sadistic, father in rural North Yorkshire. Billy realises that he has to disappear without trace because if his father ever catches up with him he will destroy him both physically and mentally. When he leaves home in the middle of the night he is badly wounded due to a series of beltings, systematically inflicted on him, by his jealous father, who used a heavy leather belt, three weeks in a row. Billy's back, buttocks and thighs were chopped to pieces and he could hardly stand up. His only method of escape was on his bicycle, towing a homemade trailer behind him. He planned his departure in such a way that he had a maximum time available before his father was able to give chase. He had no safe haven to hide in, so distance was to be his only ally, but with his badly damaged body he could only ride his bike with great difficulty and agonising pain over short distances. He called into a 24 hr roadhouse around midnight in pouring rain. It was there that his luck changed, allowing him to escape to distant pastures. He used his farming and cooking skills to embed himself into, what he hoped, was a safe haven, where he prospered with the help of the locals. His mother had forced him to learn how to cook, simple, home style meals and his father had forced him to work alongside him in the fields and meadows of the farm where he worked. Billy was astute enough to capitalise on these simple skills to make himself indispensable in his new life. He was used to working long, hard, hours in the harvest fields and root crops as well as the gardens and greenhouse at home.

ACKNOWLEDGEMENTS

I would like to dedicate this, my first attempt at a full length novel, to the members of my family who have always supported me in my various endeavours. They are always ready to pitch in at short notice to read and scrutinise each piece and check my every word. David is quite happy to deal with sudden interruptions to his work and social life to sort out technical glitches in my hardware. Thanks once again gang.

I can never forget the expertise and dedication of the team at Pick-a-woo-woo Publishing company. Without their technical skills, knowledge and persistence I would have walked away from this, very early in the piece. Writing is very hard work but I have really enjoyed this format. Thank you, everyone who has helped in any way.

Brian O'Donnell

Chapter One

Life can be and often is a mixture of savage emotions for a child growing up in a remote cottage with few friends around. Billy was born to working class parents who lived in a tied cottage in North Yorkshire. A farm labourer often had to live in a tied cottage, which was owned by the farmer who provided employment. The farm had five regular workers as well as casual help such as Italian POWs at busy times such as threshing days and potato harvesting. Billy's Dad was the only member of the team with a driving licence and basic mechanical skills enabling him to maintain the tractors and other machinery. No one else could even start the kerosene, tractors let alone drive them. Most of the work pre-war was carried out using one or more of the twelve Shire horses stabled on the farm.

By the time Billy was old enough to work with the horses there were only five left.

As soon as he was old enough to handle a horse, Billy favoured a gelding called Jack, who was jet black but he had white socks. Jack was a very obedient horse. He would always have his ears tuned to pick up the slightest call to change direction or stop without the boy having to yank on the reins. One Tuesday morning when Billy was only eight years old he was sent to the stable to get one of the horses to pull a set of harrows. He tried to harness Jack, but he was in a silly playful mood and wanted to tease the lad and lark about. He raised his head up to the roof, refusing to allow Billy to fit his collar. Billy was getting upset. He'd been told to take a horse out to the field and look sharp about it, but he had to fit the big collar around his neck. The collar was nearly as big as Billy and almost too heavy for him to lift. Just about in tears he slapped the horse on the shoulder and shouted at him, but that didn't help. In desperation Billy put the collar back on its wall hook to have a rest and Jack turned to look over his shoulder to see what

Billy was up to. Billy went back into Jacks stall and smacked him as hard as he could on his shoulder. Not that it mattered, Jack wouldn't have felt a thing but he knew Billy was mad at him. He looked up into Jacks face and yelled at the top of his voice, "You're a naughty horse Jack, a bad horse, you can stay in here all day. I don't love you any more, I hate you for getting me into trouble." Billy was puffing and panting from the effort when he had an idea. He went to the next stall took down Blaze's collar. Each horse had its own tack which had been carefully padded to suit its shape and size to prevent pressure sores. As Billy walked into Blaze's stall, she turned her head around to see what he was up to. Blaze was eager to go, to work so she held her head down low and helped him fit the collar shaking it along her neck as he rotated it into position. Jack was getting restless now, stamping his feet, whickering and whinnying in protest. Billy ignored him as he dressed Blaze for work.

Billy finished harnessing Blaze, walked her out for a drink in the trough outside the stable door then standing on the edge of the big stone trough, hopped onto her back for a ride down to the field. He could hear Jack stamping all four feet, neighing and whinnying in protest but he kept going. When Billy arrived in the field the men were keen to know why he had brought Blaze not Jack. The boss was concerned for Jack's welfare thinking he might be sick and need the vet. He asked. "Where is Jack, Billy? Is he sick or something? Why did you bring Blaze instead of Jack? Do I need to send for the vet?"

"Jack was playing silly beggars Mr Johnson," answered the lad. "He was teasing me and wouldn't let me put his collar on, and we were wasting time, so I just brought Blaze instead. Blaze can do the job just as well as Jack can't she, Mr Johnson?"

"Aha, well done lad that should teach him a lesson," replied Mr. Johnson. Blaze is a strong horse, as you say, so get her hitched up to them harrows. We've plenty of work to do, and it's late enough already. We don't want to be wasting time with temperamental horses."

The following morning Billy walked into the stable, straight past Jack's stall without saying a word to him, and harnessed Blaze. Jack kicked up a shindig, stamping, whinnying and snorting but Billy ignored him. On the Thursday morning Billy repeated the previous day's actions. Again, he harnessed Blaze and went to work leaving a sad and forlorn Jack to stare at the brick wall all day. Friday morning Billy strode masterfully into the stable saying "Now then you great, big lump are you ready to work today?" He then picked up Jack's collar off its hook on the wall and walked into the stall. Jack got down onto his front knees, turned his lowered head whilst whickering quietly, allowing Billy to slide the collar into place, turn it round and settle it comfortably on his shoulders. This mighty horse who stood eighteen and a half hands tall and weighing about a ton was humbled for all time. His head was almost as big as the boy but he knew who was the boss.

Billy was happy. Life was good out in the fields with the men and big Jack out in front, farting like mad as usual, as he leant into the work.

Both Joe and Burt the horseman were hard men and tough on their sons, Billy and Pete, who had a hard life being forced to help out on the farm and at home. Often their only reward for a job well done was a swift cuff across the ears for some little misdemeanour or omission during the day. Joe was particularly hard on Billy, blaming him for every little thing that went wrong, sometimes even when Billy had no knowledge of the event. Should Billy be stupid enough to protest his innocence he would, more than likely feel his Dad's belt across his back and backside for telling 'lies.'

One problem in their household was Billy's sister Maude, who was a couple of years older than him and inherently lazy. Maude was forever setting Billy up for a belting to cover up her own laziness. Her Dad, Joe, thought the sun shone out from her backside so she never got into any trouble. His wife, Ethel, often claimed that it was easier to do the chores herself rather than to try and get Maude to help.

On Sunday mornings in the winter Joe and one other employee, Hubert, had to work together to feed 40 or 50 fattening steers which were housed in two large, covered, fold yards. They had to start before daybreak using kerosene storm lanterns to see what they were doing. The main feed was chopped turnips and mangolds grown on the farm. There was a large engine driven chopper in the barn, which cut them into scallops suitable for the cattle. When Billy was old enough to handle the shovel to fill the scuttles used to carry the feed out into the troughs, he was dragged from his bed before daybreak to help. Once the early feed was over, the men walked back to their homes for breakfast, before returning to the fold for a second feeding of the cattle, and feeding the pigs as well, before cleaning out the pig-sties. Once the cold weather was over and the fat cattle taken to market, Joe looked forward to a lie in on Sunday mornings and he and his wife Ethel, liked a cup of tea in bed. When the children were old enough to brew a pot of tea they were told to take turns to do so.

Making a brew of tea was no easy job because there was no electricity in the cottage. The water had to be boiled on one of two, kerosene, stoves. The vaporiser had to be heated up with methylated spirits before the kerosene would ignite. Maude was never one for getting out of bed in the mornings. It was always a battle for

Billy to convince her that it was her turn. One Sunday morning Maude was determined not to get out of bed, insisting that it was Billy's turn. Billy held his ground for as long as he dared before realising his Dad would get mad and belt him if he failed to get the tea on time. His Dad would never have considered that it was Maude's turn so Billy would cop a belting. However, Maude realised that her Dad just might remember who's turn it was and she would probably get into trouble. By the time Maude arrived in the kitchen Billy was lighting one of the stoves. The methylated spirit was already burning, heating up the vaporiser. Maude, having finally got up, came down stairs and tried to take charge. She knew that if Billy took up the tea she would have to do his turn next week, which didn't seem fair since she had got out of bed early this week. Maude wrestled with Billy as he was pumping up the kerosene to ignite the main flame and in so doing knocked the stove over on its side. The remains of the methylated spirit was tipped down the front of Billy's pyjamas, setting him alight. Maude let out a massive scream as Billy wiped off the methylated spirit with a towel and squashed out the flames. Joe, on hearing his darling girl scream, jumped out of bed and rushed down stairs. Unfortunately, in his panic, forgot which way the door at the stair bottom opened and smashed into the edge of it and breaking his nose. He arrived in the kitchen with blood spurting out of his face to find that the drama was over and all was well. The terrified look on Maude's face told the tale, so amazingly, Billy didn't get the blame. Afterwards, Billy realised that his dad would have almost certainly overheard the arguments between Maude and himself as he tried to get Maude out of bed. Joe was so busy sorting out his nose that both of the kids got away without blame, he never said a word to either of them. Billy just relit the stove, none the worse for his fright. Fortunately for Billy, methylated spirit is a cold, slow burning spirit unlike petrol. Even his pyjamas were unharmed.

By the time Billy reached his early teens he was well schooled in most of the heavy tasks around the home and farm including driving the tractors but he was not strong enough to crank the brutes.

Billy's Dad used to buy in two small piglets in the early spring, which he fattened for bacon and ham for their own use as well as rendering the lard for cooking. The boss had an old, unused, pig yard and shed down in the main orchard but it was a long way from the cottage and it was Billy's job to feed the pigs there every night. It was a long haul from the house to the orchard. The food was stored near the house because all the food scraps, potato peelings and other odds and ends had first to be cooked in a metal bucket on the house fire. Barley meal was then added to make a nice tasty brew. The main road to York passed by quite close and it was on the route to the sugar beet factory in Clifton near York. The lorries carting the beets to the factory often overloaded their trucks resulting in beets falling off onto the roadside. Joe realised it could be used to feed his pigs and clean up the road as well so Billy was deployed every evening after school to collect as many as he could find to be stored in the shed then boiled up as needed each day for the pigs. Billy could only manage to fit a few beets into carrier bags on his handlebars. A single sugar beet is as big as and sometimes bigger that a rugby ball and much heavier so he visited the local scrap man where he obtained an old pram axle and wheels. These he made into a simple trailer for his bike. An old wooden crate from the grocer, a pair of old bike forks and some flat iron bar completed the picture. Joe poked a lot of 'fun' at Billie giving him a good ribbing as he often did. He had a mean sense of humour and tormented Billy constantly about girls and any other item that tickled his ego at the time. Joe steadfastly refused to help Billy, reckoning it were a waste of time building a useless trailer that he'd never be able to tow anyway, so Billy settled down to make it himself. Every night Billy went out onto the main road and filled the trailer plus the two bags on the handlebars with sugar beets which he stored in the garden shed ready to be cut into slices [another chore for Billy] and boiled in a steel bucket on the kitchen fire. Quite close to the cottage there was a very short, sharp hill which forced the lorries to change gears. The old lorries only had very crude gearboxes in those days and the resultant jerking often shook some extra beets onto the road for Billy to collect. He was able to collect enough beets to get them through the year until the next sugar beet season started. He carried out the lucrative pursuit for a few years then catastrophe struck and the beet supply ended. One afternoon one of the lorries was negotiating the hill and had to change gear with the resultant jerk which dislodged a large beet. The beet bounced off the side of the lorry and knocked a motor cyclist off his motor cycle. The rider happened to be our local Bobby [policeman], riding his police issue Francis Barnet motor cycle, who was not amused. For a number of years now all the lorries were supposed, by law, to securely tie down the beets and everything else, which they carried loose, with a suitable net or tarpaulin. From that day on the law was policed vigorously thus depriving Billy of his beet bounty.

In view of all the work carried out by Billy one would have expected his Dad to revere him or at least treat him fairly, but no, that was not to be. He still found many reasons to smash Billy across the face and head with the flat of his hands, as well as taking his belt to his backside. Not to mention the sadistic tormenting and ribbing that was a part of his daily life. Billy suspected that much of the trouble with his dad was jealousy. Joe never managed to do anything useful whilst he was at school except to write very neatly. Whereas, Billy excelled, without even trying very much. He passed the eleven plus examinations with top honours enabling him to attend the best Grammar school in the area and once there he continued to do well without too much effort. He was in the top grade and was always in the top five or six in his class.

Chapter Two

When Billy was in his early teens a social` club was established in a nearby village hall. Maude was keen to go along every Tuesday evening. Joe said she couldn't go on her own, because most of the way was along the main road to York. He said she could go providing Billy went as well, even though she was some two years his senior. Billy was keen to give the social club a go seeing as some of his classmates were regulars. As a result Billy had to rearrange his work schedule to fit the social club in. All this went well for a few weeks provided they were back home by 10.30pm. each night. The club finished at 10.00pm thus they had time to get home before the deadline.

Maude decided that she was in love with one of the village lads and wanted to spend more time in his company. A fish and chip shop had opened up at the far end of the village. This provided supper for the kids who lived in the village, providing, of course they had a few coppers left to pay for them. Maude wanted to go up there and join in the fun. No matter how much Billy argued with her she was adamant that they would have time to get some chips for their supper and still get home in time. There were quite a number of locals lined up waiting for the next batch of chips once they were cooked, and of course they were too hot to handle and eat immediately. By the time the chips were cool enough they were very late setting off home.

Billy made the big mistake and arrived home ahead of his sister. His Dad was waiting for him. There was a kitchen chair set up in the middle of the living room and when Billy hurried in his Dad grabbed him, threw him over the chair and with his belt in hand proceeded to belt the living daylights out of him. When Billy tried to explain what had happened Joe increased the assault until he was exhausted. Whilst he was in the middle of this terrible beating Maude walked past, Saying, "Good night Dad". Joe replied, "Aye, goodnight lass". Maude went up stairs to bed unscathed without even a good bollocking. When Joe's anger had been appeased he also stormed up to bed. Eventually, Billy managed to get control of his pain and crawl up the stairs on his hands and knees. Next morning in great fear of his life Billy hid in his bedroom until it was too late to walk nearly a mile or so to the bus stop. Either Joe didn't realise that Billy hadn't gone to school or maybe he realised that he wouldn't be able to walk to catch the bus to school. Even, had he got to school he couldn't possibly have sat on the hard wooden desks all day. He could hardly walk and the pain was excruciating. Amazingly Maude didn't tell her dad that he had not attended school. She loved to get him into trouble often exaggerating the order of events to get the most impact out of the situation. Tuesday came around again and Maude was keen to go to the youth club but Billy was reluctant to do so because he was still very sore from last week's beating. However, on the promise to behave, Maude persuaded him to take her. All went well on the ride to the village and they both had a good evening although Billy was still very sore. It was on the way back home that things went wrong, very wrong. Maude never looked after her bike not even to oil the chain or the wheels or even check the tyre pressure. They had no sooner set off home than her chain came off. It was far too slack and all rusty and stiff. Billy put it back on for her but it wouldn't stay on. It came off time and again so Maude had to walk most of the way home. Once they reached the cart track leading into the home stead and therefore 'safety' of sorts, Billy told her "You'll be alright now Maude so I'll race on ahead to let mum and Dad know we are safe."

As Billy stepped into the living room Joe grabbed him and started another beating whilst steadfastly refusing to listen to what Billy was trying to tell him. When Joe finally realised what Billy was saying he gave him an even bigger belting for leaving Maude behind. He said Maude was scared of the dark, [news to Billy] so he should have stayed with her. When he finally got to his room, Billy declared that, never again would he go to the rotten social club. It was far too painful.

Tuesday came around again so on the way home from the school bus, nearly a mile walk,

Billy told Maude that he was far too sore to ride his bike so he would not go to the social club. Maude whinged and grumbled but she was fairly certain her Dad would make Billy go even if he had to walk all the way. After tea Billy washed the dishes then decided to go for a long walk through the fields and woods. Walking was very uncomfortable but he needed to keep his back and legs working as much as he could and walking was the best exercise for that. He walked for a long time through all his familiar haunts until it was well passed dark and far too late to go to the club.

As he walked into his house Joe grabbed him by his ear and gave him a good bollocking for not being back to take his sister to the club. Maude put in her pennyworth complaining that she had missed out on some special events scheduled for that evening. As a result Joe whipped off his belt and gave Billy a mighty belting. Never once during all the beatings did his mother attempt to intervene and reduce the severity of the beatings. As Billy crawled up to his room he decided to escape as soon as his poor old body was recovered enough to cope with a long bike ride. On the next Tuesday he and Maude were walking home from the bus stop. The cart track left the main road dipping down slightly so that it was out of sight of the farmhouse, and Billy decided to 'sort' out his sister once and for all. He turned suddenly grabbed her and rammed her savagely into the hawthorn hedge growing beside the track. Maude shouted out, "Stop it our Billy. You're hurting me. What are you doing?"

"Teaching you a lesson our kid. You keep setting me up for a belting so I've decided to finish it. He gave her a good few hard body punches as she called out, "I'll tell Dad on you. You'll get another belting."

"I'm going to teach you a lesson, so there. We aren't going to the social club tonight or ever again and you're going to stop telling tales and getting me into trouble. You'll just have to tell Mum and Dad that we have too much schoolwork because it is near the end of term."

"You can't do this. I'm going to the club and you're taking me so there." Maude stated.

"Oh yes I can because from now on every time the old man hurts me, either with his hands or his belt I'll hurt you just like I am hurting you now." Spat Billy.

"Well I won't stand for it. You'll see when Dad gets hold of you tonight."

"You're forgetting that you're soft, whereas I'm getting used to all his beltings. He can't hurt me any more than he already has done unless he manages to kill me. Next time I will certainly end up in hospital and Dad will get reported to the police for his brutality. I've kept this lot quiet but next time I'll go straight to the hospital emergency department instead of going to school. The doctors and nursing staff will demand to know what's happened to me and report it to the police. Just think what'll happen if the old man goes to prison for assault. We'll get kicked out of the house for a start. Mr. Johnson won't put up with any of his men being charged with something as serious as, assault. Also, he'll need to find another tractor driver, even if it is only temporary, during the time the police hold Dad for questioning and the court appearances' The crops are all nearly ready for harvesting. If he can find another tractor driver he'll need our house for him. No job, no house. Make no mistake, Maude, this is only a gentle warning, next time I'll seriously hurt you. I don't care what the old pig does to me so there. We're not going to the social club ever again." Billy went straight up to his bedroom after tea and spent the whole evening studying 'Oliver Twist.

That was the end of the matter because the youth club was going into recess for the summer holidays and by the time it restarted they were living miles away. Billy enjoyed a few days of peace and calm but he knew it was only temporary.

This was the last evening of the term and by the time it reopened Billy would have disappeared. His bike and trailer went missing and were never found. His parents checked with all their relatives and friends but there was no trace of him. Billy had carefully prepared for his escape. He used some old orange boxes to make a suitable carrier to fit over the rear wheel of his bike. He could fit a small suit case horizontally on the top of the frame and strap one more on each side of the wheel. Joe had acquired a couple of ex-paratrooper's waterproof capes and Billy planned to use these to waterproof the bike and trailer. He was afraid that if he was cornered he might have to leave his trusty trailer behind at some point and fit all his stuff on the bike. He fitted most of his personal gear onto the bike and all the heavy, bulky gear such as blankets and his scout's tent in the trailer. One Friday night a couple of weeks later was 'D' day. After school Billy was ready. He knew that he must get as far away as possible that first night. He had not settled on an exact route, or a possible destination. His uncles in the coal mines of Durham County were a strong possibility. There he had a choice of two destinations, Uncle Nelson and Uncle Terrance. Both of his mother's brothers were big strong coal miners who would be able to handle his father. Furthermore neither of them had managed to sire a desperately needed son. One of the brothers had four girls whilst the other had six girls. The main problem with either of these two possibilities was, would either of them take him in and risk a family feud. This thought worried Billy and, of course, he couldn't check it out so he would have to stake his whole life and future on this huge gamble.

Billy prepared his escape well. He needed to be sure that he could make some distance before the chase began. After tea on that fateful night he sneaked out of the house and squeezed along the passenger side of the family car so that he could remove both valve cores from the tyres along with the valve core in the spare. He threw these away into a hedge. Then Billy remembered that his Dad had a box of spare valve cores in his tool cabinet in the back kitchen, these he also despatched into the hedge. The old Morris car had an add-on electric defroster/demister fitted with suction cups onto the inside of the windscreen, which he left turned on. At first he was scared that the heat from the element would melt the suction cups allowing the heater to fall down and set the car on fire. Then he thought, "What the heck, I should be miles away by then and anyway it's not my ruddy car". The idea of turning on the heater was to flatten the six volt battery was so that his dad couldn't start the engine. The Morris was fitted with a cranking handle as well as a starter motor but the SU fuel pump was electric so it needed a bit of battery power to get enough petrol to the carburettor to make the engine run. Hopefully, by the time that his dad had taken the battery to the local blacksmith's shop to be charged and hand pumped a couple of tyres up, he would be fairly safe provided his battered body could cope with riding his bike. Most of the roads around the area were quite hilly and would need a great deal of effort to get any distance. As it turned out Billy had no need to worry about any of these precautions. His immediate escape turned out to be so simple and quick that he would be many miles away before his dad woke up the next day. Joe had to work on Saturday mornings as part of his week's work so hopefully he wouldn't realise that he had any problems until after lunch.

Billy listened to hear Joe snoring late that night before loading up his bike. It took him about half an hour to get everything loaded. He decided to walk with the bike as far as the tarmac road so that he wouldn't show a light, then he was off. Once he was clear of the cart road and onto the tarmac he set off down hill in the opposite direction to the main road. The alternate road was a bit further but there were no hills in the first few miles so he made good time. If he was lucky, he would have at least twelve hours start on any pursuers.

As he approached a nearby town Billy decided to check out the huge, 24hr, transport café and filling station on the main road. The place had a massive parking area out at the rear of the buildings, which was set aside for lorries only. There were two fuel pumps out there supplying diesel fuel for the lorries with ample parking and turning space for them to manoeuvre. Billy needed a bit of a rest at that point and he was still uncertain of where he was going next. His backside was very painful already. After a short rest he finally decided to travel across the country instead of up or down to throw any followers off his scent. There was plenty of darkness left to cover his tracks so he decided to turn off and slip around the town of Barrestown on to the Leeds Road and run westwards down through the middle of the country.

He was about to move out of the car park when a huge low-loader lorry began turning into the drive way. It was fully loaded with a massive square box covered in tarpaulins. The tarpaulins didn't reach right down to the deck and Billy could see what looked like a large Electricity transformer or something similar.

In spite of his need to escape Billy couldn't help spending a little of his precious time to have a good look. He parked his little rig alongside the far wall where it was really dark then wandered over to the enormous truck. The low-loader trailer was being hauled by the biggest, Scammell, tractor he had ever seen, with another one pushing from behind He watched as the drivers pulled in close to one of the diesel pumps and began to fill the tanks. Billy could hear the drivers talking to their mates. They reckoned that they needed to fill up here to see them through the night because this was the last 24hr road house until well the south of Sheffield. They could get a good meal here as well. They were on the way to the dockside at Bristol. From there, a ship would take the transformer to Canada. The low loader was only allowed to travel at twenty miles per hour maximum so they would be travelling all night, and then all the next day as well. There were plenty of steep hills to negotiate at crawling speed and big lorries could only travel downhill in crawler gear too at the same speed as climbing up them. In fact these powerful tractors could often travel faster uphill than down them due the possibility of burning out their brakes on the decent. The crew had worked out where their next stop would be, early in the morning but it meant nothing to Billy as he had never been south of Leeds. There were only a few 24 hour roadhouses between here and Bristol and they needed one with a large enough parking area to accommodate a rig as big as this one. They had enough fuel on board, so long as the tanks were full here, to get them to Sheffield where they again had to have a maximum fill up to get through Birmingham. A quick scan of the AA handbook using the torch off his bike showed a large roadhouse complex south of Birmingham which was labelled as 24 hours 7 days per week. Quite obviously this lorry was heading for that particular roadhouse and would be there about teatime tomorrow, actually today, as it was already past midnight.

Chapter Three

Once the crew had refuelled they moved the rig over against the far wall close to Billy's outfit and facing the southbound exit to make sure no one could hem them in. The drivers and their mates went into the café for a meal and Billy moved over to get a better look at the trailer. He realised that if he undid a couple of the ropes of the tarpaulin he might just be able to get enough slack to get his bike and trailer onto the low deck as well as himself, and it would be difficult to see it hidden in there.

There seemed to be lots of room between the transformer and the gooseneck attaching the low loader onto the tractor. He quickly unhitched his trailer and lifted it onto the deck of the loader then followed it with his bike and of course himself. He could lean out from under the tarpaulin to retie the ropes, hoping that his knots would look like the other real ones. Billy then found that he could climb up onto the gooseneck where there were two or three spare tarpaulins stashed. He was going to be quite comfy up there and might even catch up on some much needed sleep. He checked that his bike and trailer were as well hidden as possible, and, short of getting down on their hands and knees on the wet ground the crew should not be able to see them. By this time Billy was totally exhausted because he had not slept well for a few nights in fact he hadn't had a decent night's sleep since the first lot of beltings. Due to all the pain of his beltings and now the excitement of his escape, he had come to a full stop. Taking his blankets from the trailer, he was sound asleep by the time the driver fired up his massive motor and headed southwards down the A1. When he stirred from his slumber the truck was negotiating a large roundabout. It was raining hard by now but he could see the big road signs as the truck pulled out of the roundabout. They were skirting the city of Leeds and heading for Sheffield. The lorry had already travelled about 35miles so he crawled back into his make shift bed and promptly went back to sleep. It was going to be a long night. It had taken more than three hours to get this far.

When next Billy awoke the diesel engine was slowing down again and more roundabouts appeared. Looking for signposts was a bit awkward but he eventually got a good look at one or two. Not being aware of the district made it difficult to find out where they actually were unless there was a big sign for a major town. It soon became obvious that the lorry was negotiating it's way around the outskirts of Sheffield. They had been on the road about six hours now and the crew would surely need to have some sort of refreshments. Billy was very hungry by then and he remembered the food that he had stashed in his school satchel. Before leaving the house he had grabbed a loaf of bread and all the fresh cakes and buns along with any biscuits that were in the pantry. There was also a decent sized lump of cheese and he had hard-boiled a few eggs when everyone was out of the house. Also there was a bag full of assorted fruit from the garden including gooseberries, apples and plums. All this would keep him satisfied for some time but he would have loved a large mug of tea. Once the men went into the café he carefully climbed out of his hidey-hole after making sure there was no one around in the parking area. He had collected all the cash from home so could pay for a nice hot drink. Whilst sitting in the café drinking his pot of tea Billy kept a careful eye on the drivers. As soon as it became obvious that they were nearly finished their meal he slipped outside again and back into his sanctuary, retying the tarpaulin carefully behind him.

Billy was aware that the distance away from his old home was increasing nicely although a little slower than he had hoped. The route now being taken was quite alien, not only to him, but to any possible chasers. His family had connections in Cowley as well as an uncle in Southsea. None of these areas were anywhere near his current route which was heading Westwards towards Bristol and the river Severn. Billy hoped to decamp some time before they got to Bristol, then hopefully, find somewhere to live and work. Another eight hours travelling should get them to the area south of Birmingham city.

Between shifts of sleeping and dozing Billy realised they were approaching the outer suburbs of Birmingham having already passed through Derby. The lorry crew were bound to stop for fuel and food somewhere soon he hoped. After Birmingham had been negotiated the road wound through more open countryside and then towards Chesterham. He realised that the best place to find work he was familiar with, such as, farming, was away from the towns. Maybe in a little village somewhere where not too many questions would be asked. He was almost fourteen now and hoped to convince people that he was actually fifteen and able to leave school to get a job. A small country village would be nice where he might find decent lodgings and employment.

Billy was surprised they hadn't stopped again before now, then he realised that there would only be a few places big enough to accommodate a huge outfit like this. Wait a minute! He also remembered the men leaving the last café carrying brown paper bags of, maybe food, like sandwiches and cans of drinks, to get them to the next oversized café, wherever that might be.

Billy had slipped his father's Automobile Association hand book in his pack just in case he needed to navigate a different route. The maps in the AA book were second to none with full descriptions of each town, as well as all the historic buildings. The light beneath the tarpaulin was not good but holding the book close to the edge of the covers he could make out most of the details of roads and services. Close to the town of Chesterham he spotted a village called Haversby and according to the AA hand book there was a large service station and restaurant/café complex near a major intersection of roads. It was his guess that this would be the next stop for a top up of fuel as well as food. They were running much later than Billy expected because when he looked out again it was dark and it was raining again. He'd hoped for a fine evening to allow time to find some sort of shelter for the night. It was after six pm by the time the lorry stopped close to the diesel pumps and began filling up the tanks. As before once the tanks were full the drivers pulled over to one side of the parking area then shut down the motors before heading for the café. Probably due to the rain, the crew didn't spend any time checking the rig over for loose chains and ropes, flat tyres or anything else. They just abandoned it and headed for the warmth of the café with their heads down against the driving rain, which suited Billy well.

He quickly undid some of the ropes pulled out his bike and parked it alongside a dark wall, then climbed back under the tarpaulin to retrieve his trailer and hooked it onto the bike. As he was tying up the ropes again a man appeared around the café wall and shone a torch around the parking area. He appeared to be some sort of security guard looking out for the lorries whilst the drivers had a meal. Sometimes if the lorry was loaded with special goods such as cigarettes and alcohol, bandits would, and still do, steal the whole rig. So the larger service stations employed security guards to safeguard the parking areas. No one was likely to steal this rig so he ran back inside the café.

Billy turned around, climbed on his bike and left the yard quickly before the man could spot him and ask any awkward questions. He went out to the front and found a suitable place to park his bike and trailer. There was a bit of cover under the roof overhang, enough to keep most of the rain off his rig. He was more than ready for a drink of tea and maybe a good feed of hot food but money was a bit short. However, he went inside the café to get a mug of tea for starters before checking his finances against the menu boards. There was a bit of a queue at the counter. The cashier was getting very angry and complaining bitterly because none of her staff had turned up for the night shift and she was on her own and in a heck of a mess as Billy could see. Some of the customers were heckling her to get her to hurry up whilst trying to explain why she couldn't supply any food nor even tea at the moment. She couldn't leave the counter, even to get a cup of tea for herself let alone visit the toilet or cook a meal She would need to have a massive sort out and clean up before she could begin to serve tea and food. Billy could see an opportunity for his own well being in all this mess. Maybe he might be able to scrounge some food as well as a hot drink without spending any of his money. He was quite happy to work for his food, even if he had to cook it himself. After all he was a competent cook due to the way he had been brought up and the time spent with his latest girl friend and classmate who lived at a classy restaurant on The A1. It appeared that this place might possibly be his salvation. He needed work and here there seemed to be work aplenty of the sort that he was used to. If he was lucky enough to get a full time job here, then his only problem would be somewhere to live. Working in a place like this would be infinitely better than working in all weathers on a farm and judging by the look and sound of things these people certainly needed some regular, reliable staff. Billy was wet through from the pouring rain, which was a great pity as he'd managed to keep dry and warm until he disembarked from the lorry. A nice warm dry kitchen would be very acceptable right now.

Chapter Four

Meanwhile, back home in Yorkshire, Billy's family had discovered that something rather odd was afoot. Ethel went into the pantry to get a loaf of bread but it had disappeared along with cakes, biscuits and the cheese. She stepped out of the pantry and shouted for Billy. Billy failed to answer even after three or four shouts, so she called Maude. Telling her to get Billy out of bed to light the fire and help her get the breakfast ready. Maude checked Billy's room and found it was empty but the bed had been set up to appear that he was still in there. She checked out the bathroom but there was no sign of Billy. Ethel then shouted at Maude telling her, "Get your bloody arse down here quick and help me for once. You're a lazy good for nothing sod and get away with things all the time."

Maude hurried down the stairs to light the kerosene stoves to start cooking. She was kicking up a stink about having to help. "It's not fair Mum. Why should I have to do it. It's our kid's job. He's supposed to light the fire not me. I'll smack his lugholes when he comes back."

Ethel went close to Maude and gave her a good slap across her face saying, "If there's any slapping to do around here I'll be doing it so shut your gob and get some work done. Did our Billy say anything to you about what he was up to."

"I haven't spoken the him since Dad gave him that last belting, which he deserved anyway. He just ignores me, but I guessed he was up to something the way he's been carrying on lately." Maude muttered between her sobs. "I bet he's gone off into the woods somewhere. Has he taken any food with him?"

"Yes, he bloody well has, half the pantry, so I'll have to get the oven hot and cook some more, quick smart before Dad gets home. Just wait till I catch up with him. Hey you, Maude, get that fire lit and stoked up while I make some bread dough. I'll need the fire to get the dough to rise properly"

"Oh heck this is crazy Mum." Maude called out from the living room, "How can I light the fire? The lazy beggar hasn't even brought any kindling in nor any wood or coal. The coal bucket's empty how am I supposed to get a fire going?"

"Well don't just stand there. Get outside and get some kindling from the shed then set the fire. Once you get it going you can bring in some small logs then a bucket of coal. I expect you to have a good hot fire by the time this dough is ready unless you want another crack across your face. Our Billy has done all this for years without a single grizzle and he's younger than you, so stop your complaining and do something useful for a change."

Gradually, the women got the household going again. Maude soon had a good fire going. Ethel had a bowlful of bread dough proving in the hearth in front of it. Whilst waiting for the bread she started making up pastry for pies and dough for scones. If only Billy could have seen them he would have had a good old laugh. By the time Joe got home for his dinner the kitchen was more or less back to normal and there was a decent meal sitting on the table waiting for him. Ethel asked Joe, "Have you any idea what our Billy's up to, Joe, we can't find him any where? He's taken a whole lot of food with him an' all,"

Maude added "I bet he's run away. He's probably gone to Boston." Joe's mother and sister both live in Boston Spa.

"Like I always said, he'll come home when he gets hungry." Joe said. "Is my dinner ready yet because I'm starving? As soon as I've had a bit of dinner I'll get t'car out and we'll run over to Boston and see Mum. She might have some idea where the rotten little sod is hiding"

When Joe had eaten his dinner he opened the garage doors but when he looked in he could see the car was leaning to the passenger side. He checked the tyres and was amazed that both passenger side tyres were flat. "I must have run over summat in yard with both wheels" he said to himself. "I bet our Billy has left something sharp lying about. I'll kill the sod when we find him." He went round the driver's door and got in, sat down and put the key in the ignition. When he pulled out the starter nothing happened. The battery must have gone flat as well. He squeezed down the side, checked, then removed the battery. He went back indoors to tell Ethel what had happened and he was ropeable. "I'll have to take the bloody battery up to Perry Styan and get it charged up again, I got two bloody flat tyres an' all. I need the battery to get the car out cause I can't get down the passenger side to change either of the wheels or get to pump 'em up. I'll 'ave to take your old bike with the kids seat to put the battery on. Damn that bloody Billy. Just let him wait til I get a hold of 'im.

Joe went into the bike shed only to find Billy's bike gone and the carrier was missing off Ethel's bike as well. It was one that he had made when Maude was small so Ethel could take her on the back. Billy, of course, had removed the box from his Mum's bike and used it as a base to build up a carrier for his own bike.

All this drama left Joe with only one choice. He had no option. He mounted his bike, then balanced the battery on his crossbar for a trip to the blacksmith shop. He decided to go the other way though, to Henry Styan in Ormsby because there were no hills in the way, but it was about twice as far to go.

Henry had a rapid charger and soon had the battery working again. He offered to run Joe back home with the battery, which Joe was glad of. Once the battery was in place Joe carefully reversed out of the shed so that he could get at the wheel studs and Jack up the car. Surprise, surprise, guess what? No valve cores. That's when Joe began to realise what Billy had done to him. He took out the spare wheel only to find that not only was it flat but it had no valve core either. By now Joe was crazy mad at Billy. Let's hope Billy was far enough away because murder would have been done that day. After storming around the yard and yelling at Ethel and Maude, he remembered the spare valve cores in the tool cabinet. He opened the tool cabinet and he was savage when he found the little red box had gone, along with the valve cores. This meant another trip to the local garage to get more. Time was getting on and the garage shut at five o'clock. God help that bloody Billy when he found him. Joe did eventually get the car going just in time to go to Boston but his mother had no idea that Billy would do a runner or where he would go. She was furious with Joe when she was told some of the story. She said, "It served Joe right and she hoped they didn't find Billy again, not ever. Joe said, "Aye well you might 'ave a point, Ma. I'll just pop next door to our Emily's. She might have heard summat. When I come back we'll just have a nice cuppa and get going. I've just 'ad a thought though. Our Billy was great friends with a lad in Barrestown. He often stayed at their place on the housing estate. Them two lads were allus together. When Billy wasn't at Tony's place for the weekend, they were both at our end. If anybody knows ow't about job it'll be Tony.

Joe went to see his sister Emily but she had no idea that Billy was even missing, let alone where he could be. Joe returned to his mother's cottage for a welcome cup of her really strong tea with some Caraway seed cake as well. They had missed out on afternoon tea and now it was almost time for his tea. In rural Yorkshire, dinner, [hot meal] was always at 'lunch' time, midday, and tea was the evening meal.

Barrestown was about twelve miles away from Boston but quite a nice drive. The old Morris soon ate up the miles and they stopped outside number 16 Meadow, Court. Joe jumped out and knocked on the front door. Mrs. Skotchdale opened the door with a look of surprise on her face, "Now then Joe, are you looking for our Tony?"

"Aye well sort of." Joe replied, "Actually I'm looking for our Billy. I thought he might have come here to you, like, he's disappeared. We thought Tony might have some idea what he was planning to do. Your lad and him were always great pals so I was hoping he might have some idea what he was going to do. We think he might have run away like, you know, left 'ome or summat. Is your Tony still at home, here?"

"Oh heck, Joe, you'd better come in and tell us all about it. Is Ethel with you, bring her in as well, she must be very upset. I'll just give our Tony a shout he's working in the shed. He is trying to fix a television set for a friend of ours"

Tony and the rest of the Skotchdale family couldn't offer any help so Joe headed off home to have a good think about the situation. When they arrived home Ethel remarked, "I was thinking about our Nelson and Terence. I know it's a long way to ride, but there are no big hills along theA19. He would still be hurting like mad so he might have holed up somewhere along the way. He was always very resourceful like that. He learnt a lot of stuff in the scouts as well. Maybe if we leave it until next weekend, would that give him time to get there? We could drive there on Sunday morning and catch up with our Nelson and Terence."

"Aye well, he's got me stumped. I've thought of everything. So, let's get some tea on and worry about him later. With all this mucking about I'm fair buggered and so hungry I could eat a horse. Come on Maude shape yourself and give Mum a hand. I'll get a nice fire going. You two can light the primus stoves and get a frying pan on the go. There's bound to be plenty of eggs and sausages in the pantry. There's still heaps of bacon and ham hanging up in there as well". As soon as I get a fire going and some nice coals I'll get busy with the toasting fork. Mum will have plenty of bread that only needs slicing. Grab the bread and butter as you come out of the pantry. Between us we won't starve. We'll have a feed on the table in a few minutes. See if you can find a tin of baked beans or summat that we can heat up as well.

Chapter Five

Back at the roadhouse with no awareness about the drama back home, Billy tried to get a word in edgeways to the cashier. She was trying to ignore him as she sorted out other problems. There was no one in the kitchen and from where Billy was standing he could see piles of dishes everywhere. The previous shift had obviously just left at 6 o'clock leaving everything in a mess for the next shift, who, hadn't turned up. Every available space was piled up with dirty dishes and cutlery, saucepans and cooking utensils. Billy pushed in and spoke to the lady saying, "Excuse me missus, if I get stuck in and clear up that mess in the kitchen for you, can I get a feed please. You see, I'm really hungry. I'm really good at washing up and sorting out a mess like that and I'm running short of money so we could help each other if you'll let me."

The lady was about to brush Billy off with some rude words for jumping the queue and butting in when she was so busy. She had no time to deal with a smart arsed kid at the moment. Then she realised what he was saying and she was quite desperate. He might just be her salvation for time being anyway. Without hesitation she said. "I'm not promising you anything but if you do a good job in there, I'll see you right, Ok? Before you get started fill up both of those urns and switch them on again, then see if you can brew some tea. I'm nearly out of clean cups and mugs as well."

Billy stripped off his wet outer clothes, rolled up his sleeves and made a start. He noticed that the big kettle on the stove was boiling so he tipped the dregs out of one of the big teapots, splashed a little of the boiling water into the teapot to heat it up. He stuck his head out of the hatch asking the lady, "Where do you keep the tea and how much do you put in the big teapot?"

"Look over there near the first urn there should be a large tin with kittens painted on it. Just stick your hand in and that should be enough, as much as you can fit in to your hand will do.

Billy did just that then added a bit more because his hands were a bit small. Once the tea had brewed he took it out to the counter for the lady who was surprised to see it so soon. "Was the water really hot enough to make tea young man, we need it to brew properly? The water has to be boiling hot"

"Aye of course it was, the kettle was bubbling and I warmed the pot first"

Billy set to and got to work. He had to empty one of the sinks and drainers on to the floor to get enough room to operate and from then on it was straight forward. Then the lady stuck her head through the hatch saying, "I don't suppose you can rustle up three or four mixed grilles, can you? Can you cook at all mate?" If you make a start on them I'll come in and finish them off. Just get the frying pans going and make some toast to go with a mug of tea to get started.

"No problem" he replied "Where will I find all the stuff to cook?

"Have a look in that cold room over on that wall. See what you can find. Then have a look in that big pantry cupboard next to it. I'm in such a mess here with my bloody staff not showing up that I don't know what there is. Just use your imagination. Let's see what you can come up with but bloody hurry up. Lorry drivers don't like waiting. Time is money to them blokes and they only want to get home to their families."

Billy had just washed up a couple of large frying pans, which he put on the stove along with dripping from the pantry. The first things he came across were some sausages so he threw eight of those in one of the pans with a heap of bacon rashers, which he cut in two halves with a pair of scissors. The other pan he loaded with eggs then he needed some mashed taties to build up the centre of the dishes. He needed a substitute for now. He had spotted a large catering size tin of Heinz Baked Beans, They would have to do. If he put in a large serve of them they should fill up the truckies and make them happy. He put a good quantity into a saucepan with a heavy dash of Worcester sauce to heat up. Billy cut some very thick slices of bread from a catering size loaf and set them to toast. He found a dish of butter and four large plates and he was in business.

When the food was well cooked he delivered it out to the drivers along with masses of toast and pint-sized mugs of tea. Back in the kitchen it was all go. More and more cups of tea were needed even the odd cup of coffee [instant]. There seemed to be quite a lot of assorted, nondescript ingredients in the pantry so Billy got out a large boiling pan, added quantity of water and salt before chopping and feeding in to it any useful looking vegetables. He found carrots, parsnips, onions, leeks, suedes, celery, turnips and potatoes. Most of these were a bit shrivelled and passed their best dates but admirable to boil up into soup and clear out the pantry at the same time. Now he could see what was left in there. The boss would need to order in fresh stocks in the morning but at least now she would be able to see what was needed. Next he would need some sort of meat to make a nice juicy stock, preferable something with plenty of bones.

In the cool room there were some forequarter mutton chops which needed using up soon and even ancient but still ok steak bits, some older bacon rashers and a great prize to finish it off. There was a large ham bone with a decent quantity of meat left on the knuckles and lots of marrow in the centre. Hopefully by about midnight Billy would be able to serve his own brand of homemade soup with lots of crusty bread. There were two large stockpots and enough ingredients to fill them both.

The café was very busy even though it was Saturday night with many of the lorries already off the road for the weekend. It was around 2.30 am before things eased off a bit and the boss lady came back into the kitchen for a chat. This was it for Billy, do or die. He didn't want to tell a lot of lies to cover his arse but he would need to resort to some fibs to get him through this interview. It wouldn't take much to bring out the hounds again. He had vowed to stab himself in the heart with his boy scouts knife and end his miserable life quickly rather than submit to any more painful beltings, Having passed his first aid exams recently at scouts he knew exactly where to find his heart and had already considered this action if his escape bid failed.

Having decided to 'come clean' with his new

boss he was prepared for the interrogation. The Boss lady introduced herself as Vanessa Riley.

To try and keep his secrets Billy became 'Billy The Kid', with a promise of more detail later on if the situation warranted it. Without letting out too much detail for now Billy explained that he had escaped from a home of hell and was, 'on the run' so to speak. He explained that he needed shelter of some sort and a reasonable job to make ends meet, and buy new clothes. He said that he was prepared to work hard for a fair wage. Vanessa for her part said that she was really amazed at the work Billy had gotten through already that night without any help.

Vanessa said, "I'm amazed at how you have coped tonight Billy, especially as you got off to a very bad start. If the other crew had measured up it would have been easy. I usually have a cook and kitchen hands as well as a waitress at night. The amount of work you got through already, your ability to run the kitchen and serve as well shows great promise for the future. You're a good cook for one so young. Your mother must have taught you well. The lorry drivers enjoyed your mixed grilles asked me to thank you. They said if you had had more time for preparation they thought it would have been even better. They pointed out that when they are on the road they are at the mercy of roadhouse cooks. Sometimes it works out well as it did tonight but some roadhouses just make monkeys of them using poor quality ingredients, bad cooking skills, and horrible table service as well a charging like mad. They've vowed to return and get your roster days so that they can call in regularly and bring their pals. That, of course, leaves us with a number of problems to sort out between ourselves."

"Firstly, do you want to stay around and work here with me?" Billy replied, "YES please if I can find somewhere to live, that is."

"Then I need to find you accommodation, but I can do that easily, at my place. "How do you feel about working nights and weekends only?"

Billy replied "Yes, please, double time means more money in my pocket."

"Then there is your age. How old are you Billy?"

Billy replied "My next birthday is in a few weeks time on the fifth of September, which is before the next school term starts. Billy didn't lie about his age, just missed out a year. He just inferred that he would be of legal age to leave school in September.

"So, how much do you think you are worth, young man?"Asked Vanessa.

"Quite a lot, actually." Said Billy. "You said I did more work tonight than your cook, kitchen hands and a waitress put together so if we add all their wages together we should be close to working out my worth and I'll work harder than the whole lot of them put together." Vanessa had to have a good giggle at that but didn't agree or disagree. "That leaves one problem. Do I have a vacancy suitable for an overnight blow in, who's a smart arsed, cheeky, monkey who can cook quite well and run my kitchen?" asked Vanessa. "Yes, ok, but only time will tell me the answer to that."

Some rearrangements will need to be made though. After tonight's effort I need to attend to that urgently, anyway. I have customers coming in now so we'll leave it there for now. Is that ok Billy, think it over? I'll be back, just carry on what you're doing"

"It sounds as though you have all avenues

covered boss so, yes thank you. Do I call you Vanessa, Boss, Ma'am or whatever?"

"How about 'Boss' around here,"

Billy followed Vanessa into the counter area asking, "Do you have an order book for supplies or a note book, or even some paper and a pencil?" He asked.

"There should be an order book on the shelf next to the pantry door. Make sure you put different types on new pages. Let's say the butcher, baker, green grocer, co-op stores. That should do it for a start and make life a bit easier, later on at the shops."

"Ok, I'll get started now all the mess is gone.

The rest of the night was quite busy although it was early Sunday morning and there was plenty to do especially in the kitchen. It seemed as though the kitchen was long overdue for a major clean up. Everything was quite grotty and some areas disgusting. Whilst keeping quite busy making teas and toast and more soup Billy found time to tackle the worst areas. He was amazed that the local health inspector allowed it to get that dirty without him jumping on someone. By the time 6.00

am was approaching there was still plenty to do but all was ready for the next shift. Vanessa stuck her head into the kitchen and called out to Billy, "I'm off to sort out some staff problems before any more customers arrive. I shouldn't be very long, then, we'll sort out where you will be living. Mary runs the day shift, counter and till. Here she is now." Sure enough, a middle aged woman entered the rear door through the kitchen, pulling off her coat as she did so and complaining bitterly about the rain, put her bag under the counter before balancing the till and counting the change. She eventually turned and finally greeted Billy, saying "I'm Mary, who the hell are you? What's a kid like you doing in here?"

"My name's Billy. Vanessa has given me a job here in the kitchen."

"Ok, that's good then. You can start by making me a good strong cup of tea."

"Yes Maa-aam." Billy replied, cheekily. "Coming up."

Oh my god! What sort of a bitch have we got here, he wondered as he attended to her requests. No wonder they are having staff troubles. A couple of car drivers came in through the front doors and since no one had arrived to work in the kitchen Billy was told to attended to their needs. As he was clearing their table the rear door opened to admit a very sorry looking young woman. She appeared to still be drunk and about to be violently sick all over his nice clean kitchen, which she was. Billy grabbed a bucket from the store room but he was too late to collect the bulk of the mess. Then Mary stuck her head through the door in disgust shouting out to the boy, "Don't just stand there. boy. Go get a mop and clean that mess up then you can cook me some breakfast. Poach two eggs and make sure they are nice and runny. Fry two rashers of bacon and make plenty of toast. I'm starving. Billy cleaned up the worst of the vomit before attending to the breakfast order."

The girl sat in a corner with the bucket moaning and groaning. She was as white as a sheet and shaking like a dog shitting razor blades. They were not going to get any sense, let alone help from her today. Just as the meal was about ready another woman entered the rear door threw off her coat saying, "I'll have another of them kiddo that looks really good." She went straight through to the counter area and flopped on a chair, declaring, "Hey! Mary I'm absolutely buggered. We danced most of the night. We came straight here after that. I haven't been to bed yet. Me and George had a good old shag in his bloody old ford car. It was murder. I think my back must be broken. It hurts like hell. We'd better not be busy today I'd never cope." She settled down in the chair to have a good old natter with Mary before polishing off her breakfast, belching loudly and dumping the dishes on the counter for Billy to wash. "It's still raining cats and bloody dogs out there."

Presumably the daytime cook was still to come, thought Billy but it's almost seven o'clock already. Mary started yelling at him again demanding food and tea for the next lot of customers, but Billy had had enough of these witches, he was getting out of there, fast. He collected his outer clothing from the hooks behind the door and pulling on his coat, walked out. He wiped the seat of his bike to dry it, climbed on and rode out onto the southbound roadway. He didn't care where he went just so long as he got out of there. One thing was certain though he wouldn't be able to get very far because he was exhausted, He would have to lookout for any old buildings so that he could get out of this incessant rain and try to get some sleep. After about a mile or so he spotted a small deserted looking farmyard with a decent barn and some horseboxes. The big barn looked ok but it was a bit big and draughty. There was some straw for bedding if he couldn't find anything else more comfortable. Next he checked out the nearest loose horsebox which looked as though it hadn't been used for many months, maybe even years. There was a semi circular manger across the back wall with plenty of straw and hay around. Billy took off his wet coat and hung it up on a convenient nail in the wall to dry off a bit before digging into his luggage and pulling out a couple of heavy grey ex-army blankets and a heavy woollen sweater. He pulled the sweater over his head and snuggled into its warmth then laid out one of the paratrooper capes and a blanket across the manger and crawled beneath the other one. Sore and aching though he was Billy was a sleep in no time.

Vanessa had been held up in her search for suitable staff, willing to work at weekends. She had first visited the homes of last night's cook and kitchen hands where she told them not to come again. They were fired on the spot. The young waitress lived out of town a little way and was hard to find. She claimed to be very sick and was going to see her doctor on the next day, Monday. The cottage where she lived with her parents didn't have telephone connected to call in sick. Her father was a long distance lorry driver and had only returned home over night. This all meant that she at least was still employed once she was well enough to work again.

With sick and tired workers sorted Vanessa needed to check out her emergency names to find replacements. Her efforts were not completely successful although she had some success. Thank goodness Billy had turned up to help fill some of the gaps, She got a big shock when she arrived back at the café to find one staff member vomiting in the kitchen and one other sitting out at the counter chatting to the only staff member still working. Mary was going to have to carry the full load by herself until Vanessa could arrange for others to come in.

Once all that was settled, sort of, anyway, Vanessa looked around for Billy. When it was obvious that Billy wasn't around any more she asked Mary, "Where the heck is Billy, I can't see him anywhere?"

Mary snapped, "Who the heck's Billy when he's at home then?

"The young man who was here when you came on, remember?"

"Oh, that useless little dickhead. he made a couple of meals for us and a few teas, that's all. Where the hell did you get an idiot like that from? Why the hell is he hanging around here? When I told him to put up a couple of breakfast plates for the customers he spat the dummy and walked out."

"Shit Mary you're in one of those moods again are you?" Vanessa admonished her. "Billy is on my staff not yours. He worked a full night shift on his own. None of my staff came in last night so I put Billy on. The place was in a terrible mess after your mob left last night, when he walked in looking for a temporary job so I started him straight away. He cleaned up all your mess, then ran the kitchen and wait staff single handed for twelve hours and you, smart bitch that you are, chased him away. He was only waiting for me to collect him and organise somewhere to live, so that he could stay around. Did you see where he went? The poor little bugger must have been exhausted."

Elizabeth jumped up at last saying, "Hey Mary, remember, those people from up north, the woman with a squeaky, Durham accent came in and pointed out that weird looking bike outfit heading onto the main road. He had some sort of trailer fastened behind the bike. None of us had ever seen anything like it at all. Anyway he was heading off down South, by the way he took off. It was raining like hell. It was hard to make out what it really was."

"Well he won't have got very far. He must have been totally exhausted. You should have seen how much work he got through. At least you would have had a clean start in a clean kitchen and all the crockery and utensils in their proper places. There was heaps of soup ready to serve, the urns all full and tea on the go."

"Yea that was alright until that bitch Alice turned up and spewed all over everything. She was blind drunk and still is by the look of her. Billy found a bucket for her to spew into then set about cleaning up the mess. It still stinks of vomit in there. Somebody will have to set on an clean it all up." Said Elizabeth.

"There you go then, Elizabeth, that's your first job, after you kick that silly cow out of there. Thank you, for volunteering to help. It's nearly 8 o'clock already and nothing's done yet. You just make dammed sure that you clean up all that puke and get rid of the stink." Said Vanessa. "I'm going out now to see if I can find that boy. You lot had better hope like hell that I find him and he is safe and well otherwise you'll all be in the dole queue tomorrow morning and I might yet put some of you out there anyway."

Vanessa and the local cops were best buddies and always ready to assist each other where possible so she picked up the telephone and called the desk sergeant to put him in the picture and request the help of the force to scour the area. He promised that his staff would keep a good look out for Billy and he thought that the unusual bike and trailer arrangement would be a great help, if it turned out to be him. Vanessa then jumped in her panel van and drove south out of town. She calculated that Billy couldn't possibly have travelled far even if he was fully fit which he certainly was not at the moment. She travelled up and down each road heading southwards without a sign of him. As she drove along she tried to remember everything that had been said between the two of them in the short time they were together. She passed an old stone barn close to the roadside a couple of times before she put it all together. Billy talked about his plan to live rough in the countryside if he needed to. He'd told her about his little boy-scout tent and other equipment. Then mentioned camping under the stars if the weather was fine or hopefully find a barn or other farm shed if he thought it might rain.

Vanessa returned to the café and phoned the police to tell them what she could remember of their conversation then set off again, stopping near and searching each farm shed and barn. Then she got lucky, the second barn that she looked in showed some promise so she began checking the loose boxes nearby and there he was sound asleep. It was his bike and trailer parked along one wall that gave him away. She opened up the van lifted Billy out of the manger and carefully settled him in the passenger seat. He never moved a muscle as she wrapped him up in his blankets.

Just then one of the police cars pulled up and the officers helped her to load Billy's bike and trailer into the van. The sergeant was amazed to see the trailer outfit. Then he asked, "How did you manage to get him out and into the car?"

"Oh that was the easy part said Vanessa, "The boy is as light as a feather. He's just skin and bone. I'll have to start feeding him up when I get him home. He said he would work just for a good meal but I never checked to see if he actually did eat anything. He was surrounded with food so I just assumed that he would have helped himself, which he may have done, probably picked all night I shouldn't wonder."

"Ok, now, where do we go, Vanessa?" Asked the sergeant.

"Oh that's quite simple sergeant, I'll carry on with my original plan,"

"That's ok for now my girl, but I'll have to fill in my report back at the police station."

"Yes of course mate, silly old me. I didn't get around to telling you all the facts. I need Billy to work for me at the roadhouse and he has agreed. The only thing we didn't manage to set up for him, was, where he will live whilst he's working for me? I told him that was the simplest bit but I never got the chance to explain the details to him before we got busy again thanks to my shit awful staff or ex-staff as they may become. I have decided to let him stay with me in the farmhouse, if that's ok with you. As you know my house is huge with five bedrooms, attics and all sorts interesting nooks and crannies. He told me that he comes from a farming background and always been forced to help out on the farm. He's a keen gardener as well. He can even drive a tractor so that should be very handy around the farm and keep him happy, and out of trouble."

"Ok Vanessa you appear to have everything under control so I'll let you get him home and settled after a nice hot bath and a warm bed. I forget you've had a long arduous night as well especially with your staff troubles. Hell, how would you have coped without Billy Boy to hold your hand?"

"Oh! I would have closed the kitchen down for the night and just sold fuel at the front." Vanessa replied. "You should come in and have a mug full of soup to taste it on your way out. Billy has brewed up more soup for the day shift. He makes excellent soup and it's a very cold morning outside. You need some hot soup to warm you up."

"I would like to keep a close eye on him as he settles in with you. I'll have to interview him formally to keep the record straight. It will be very interesting to see what he has to say but I will keep it as informal as I can. I understand from what you've told me, little enough though it is, that Billy won't be willing to tell us too much. However, I will pop into the café a bit more often to check up on his progress and try to get to know him better. On the days that you are both off shift I might even call in at your house in plain clothes for a chat and a cuppa. We should soon be able to get some sort of a story out of the lad. Any secrets that he may have will be safe with me but I do need to understand the background of his story just in case there are any repercussions later on. Once I can understand what caused all this upheaval, I should be able to put together some sort of a story to cover our backsides. We don't want to end up getting into trouble for kidnapping, do we? I may then be able to help out where I can if there is any sort of official enquiry. Say mate, I'm due for a break about now so I'll take you up on that mug of soup, ok. That's the best we can do for him now so I'll say good day to you and thank you for all your help. Maybe it would be wise to visit informally in plain clothes the first time. Good bye Vanessa."

"I'll give you a ring as soon as he wakes up this afternoon. Goodbye Sergeant, see you soon. And, Sergeant, thanks again for all your assistance. Have a good day."

Chapter Six

Vanessa drove home, which, as she stated was a smallish farm situated behind the village and sitting along the banks of The River Avon with a railway running nearby Judging by the size of the house and homestead, the farm had been much larger and most of the land had been sold off leaving a sizeable strip with the house wrapped within it, along the banks of the River. The front driveway was only about a mile away from the roadhouse with a tarred road right passed the gateway. She parked behind the house in a gravelled yard close to the rear entrance to the house. She went inside opened several doors and set up some pillows on a gigantic settee in the drawing room then returned to get Billy who was still sleeping soundly. Vanessa carefully lifted him out of the seat of her van and carried him gently into the house settling him among the pillows on the settee. Billy hardly stirred. He only moaned a little and grunted as he was moved then settled again as she threw a rug over him.

Vanessa hoped that he would sleep as long as possible until about 4.00 pm giving her time to organise, and air a bed for him, get him into a bath and sort out the best of his clothes before she had to get back to the roadhouse. If yesterday was any example she would have to be early at the café to sort out any problems there before she took over the reins around 6.00 pm. The next job for her was to refresh the slow combustion stove for cooking dinner and more importantly getting lots of hot water for baths and laundry. Normally when she was on her own the hot water heater in the slow combustion was adequate for her needs. She had only to stock the firebox with slow burning coke and it would last all night. By the smell of Billy's clothing it was long overdue for a good soaking before a thorough wash cycle. He would need to have a shopping event sooner rather than later as most of his stuff was old, tattered and patched. At least he would soon be in funds to enable him to buy up a new outfit. She reckoned that he would be too proud to accept any charity but she could outfit him for work with a uniform from the café running funds. Maybe she could even make him look like a chef.

It was slightly after 4.00pm when Billy flicked open his eyes and look around with horror. Where was he? Who had grabbed him? What should he do to escape again? Where was his bike and trailer? Just then Vanessa walked into the room with a big smile on her face. "Are you hungry pal or do you feel like a nice hot bath first. I have stoked up the stove so we have plenty of hot water and two fluffy towels waiting for you. Shall I run you a bath first?"

"Where are we, Vanessa? How did I get here? Who knows where I am?"

"Ok mate fair enough. When you escaped from the café it was pouring rain but someone went in to the café and told Mary about a funny bike thingy which seemed to be towing a trailer. Because the visibility was so bad the lady wasn't all that sure what she had seen except that it went south. When I went back to the café I asked where you were. Mary was ropable because she thought you were day staff not night staff and she had no idea that you had just worked a twelve hour night shift with me, not to mention that you had been travelling all day as well. She thought you had just skived off because you were a lazy beggar and didn't want to work. That aside however, Elizabeth remembered the woman with a squeaky voice telling them about the bike heading off down south.

"That was all I needed to start me off. I rang my friend at the police station and described what I thought might have been your bike rig. The Sergeant is a good friend of mine so he offered to help find you. I set off southwards away from here. I reckoned that you would be exhausted so would not have got very far but there was no sign of you. I tried all the south roads them remembered the remark about sleeping rough like a boy scout. I soon found you in a horsebox sound asleep. Don't look so worried the Sergeant is an old mate of mine. He has promised to keep your secrets, whatever they are. You are well and truly safe mate. This is my house and you are welcome to stay here for as long as you need to or want to. Now what about that bath, you'll soon feel better after a good soak."

Vanessa went upstairs to the main bathroom, ran a bath, put in some bath salts to ease any discomfort he might have, put two bath size towels on the rail ready. She persuaded Billy up stairs into the bathroom and started to help him get his outer clothes off. He became very uneasy about Vanessa's presence, which was not surprising for a boy of his age however he had difficulty removing his sweater and shirt so she had to help. Billy's vest was stuck to his back so she left him to get undressed telling him to leave the vest until he had soaked it in the bath. She left him to himself for a little while then hearing sounds of distress and maybe sobbing she popped her head back in to make sure he was coping. Billy was lying down in the bath crying his eyes out. He was terribly upset and shivering madly.

She asked him gently, "Would you like me to help you with your vest Billy? Why are you getting so upset? Why don't you tell me about it matey?

He began to tell her some of his story, "My Dad has been belting me so much that he cut my back and bum to pieces I thought the cuts had stopped bleeding and healed a bit before I left home, but the scabs must be sticking my vest and trunks onto my skin. It hurt like mad when I tried to get undressed I hoped the warm water would soften the scabs so I can get my vest off."

"Oh heck, you poor little mite let me help you. Just yell out if it hurts too much." Slowly, steadily, gradually she eased the vest upwards. She stopped to give the boy a rest while she collected a pair of scissors. Very carefully, Vanessa cut up both side of the vest. The front just fell off out of the way then she started lifting the back panel off. She could see the problem now. Blood had soaked into the vest then the scabs had stuck it all together. She said, "Now Billy I want you to be very brave. It will hurt a bit but I will be as gentle as I can. Some of these cuts will probably open up again and may bleed a bit. Don't worry if it does because I will dress them up again. I was a fully trained hospital nurse before I took on the roadhouse so I know what I am doing. I am just hoping that none of them are infected. By the smell of them I think they may be. I have some really good antiseptic cream that will heal it up quickly." With that she quickly pulled off the vest. Billy shouted out but it was all over now. Some of the cuts were a little infected but not too badly so and there was very little bleeding, just a little seepage here and there, thank goodness. Vanessa thought that she might have to take the boy to the doctor or the hospital for some antibiotic treatment which would have caused all sorts of problems for Billy with the authorities. She had to cut down both sides of Billy's trunks then she said, "Ok mate we have to do this next bit but I will be very gentle. I need you to lean forward and rest on your knees then I can see how much damage he has done to your bum, alright. Just hang in there pal it's nearly done."

"Ok Vanessa, I'll try not to yell out." Said Billy, as he rolled forward onto his knees. His bottom was not anywhere near as bad as his back. Probably due to rubbing on the bike seat, it was quite loose and easily peeled off. Most of the scabs were good and clean so would soon heal. Vanessa left Billy to finish off his bath in private and she went down stairs to assemble a set of clothes for him to wear from his meagre wardrobe. She checked the medicine cabinet and found some healing ointment as well as some anti-inflammatory cream to ease his bruises. Once she had treated all his wounds he dressed himself and they went down to have a nice meal. Normally on working days Vanessa did not eat at home. She waited until she got to the café. Tonight however she had a large pot of meaty stew for them to share. By the time they had cleaned up it was time for work. Vanessa tried hard to get Billy to stay home but he insisted on going in to help. He said, "I have to come with you to help out and earn my keep, Vanessa. You have been so kind to me, thank you for your help."

"You shouldn't be working with all those sores mate. I won't allow it" Vanessa declared. Don't you worry about paying for your board because you earned enough last night to last you a month at least.

Billy was just as stubborn insisting that he

had to go. "I'm ok Vanessa I need to keep on working so I don't have time to think and worry about what's happened to me, and what might still be to come in the future, so please let me help in the café again tonight."

"Ok then soldier, come along with me, but please remember, if any of it gets too hard for you just say so and stop."

As they were leaving through the kitchen door Billy turned to Vanessa asking, "Vanessa please, what happened to my bike and trailer? Is it still in that stable? Can we go and get it please?"

"There is no need to worry about your bike pal, the Sergeant helped me to put it in my van and I brought it home here. They are safely tucked away in one of my barns where no one will see them, but I took the liberty of sorting through your belongings and I have soaked and washed the best of them. Tomorrow we'll go to see a dear friend of mine and get you a set of new clothes to wear in the café. I can't have my head chef looking like a tramp, now can I? They both got in the Van and set out for work. When they arrived at the café Vanessa suddenly remembered her promise to the

Police Sergeant. She put a call through and apologised to Terence, the sergeant, pointing out that she had been so stressed and worried about Billy and clean forgot. Terence replied, telling her not to worry any more. He had fixed everything at his end so the missing boy incident was only a mistake and all was well. Then he said, "Is it possible for me to come round and chat with Billy for a few minutes. I just need to get this all under my belt so to speak?"

"Yes of course, pal, we are at work in the café. If you are nice to Billy you might even get a mug of tea for your trouble. I've told him about your part in his rescue so it will be ok. Just be gentle with him. When Terence arrived he entered the kitchen nice and quietly saying, "Now then young man, how is our hero today. Did you get a good sleep?" Then turning round he pointed out his colleague who had come with him. He introduced her saying, "Billy this is WPC Mabel Jones she works with me in my office, and this Mabel is our latest citizen, Billy the Kid."

She said, "I am very pleased to meet you Billy. I have been hearing all about your good deeds here in this very kitchen. I like your name for now, but when we get to know you better I am sure you will be happy to share your real name and other details with us." Poor Billy he was dumbfounded. This was all too much for him and he could feel another round of tears building up behind his eyes, but he managed to say, "I'm pleased to meet you both and thank you for all your help last night. I imagine that I'll see a fair bit of you both in the days to come. I have a ton of work waiting for me here now so I'll say cheerio for the time being and get on with my work."

The police went back into the café and congratulated Vanessa for helping Billy. They were having some difficulty believing what they had just witnessed. Billy carried off the interview with great aplomb and poise. They didn't realise that he was presently having a quiet little weep in the pantry where no one could see his distress. Vanessa stopped the ceremony with the words, 'Thank you Terence but there is a lot more to come and I along with Billy will need your help before this can all be laid to rest. "You see, Sergeant," Said Vanessa becoming very formal. "Billy has been very badly beaten.

I managed to get his clothing off and put him in a warm bath. I have treated all his wounds for now but we can't afford to report it officially and expose his whereabouts. You will have to trust me with this one please. However, I would like the two of you to visit my home in the next day or so and get Billy to relate some of his story and show you his back and buttocks. I want you both to see the mess that his father has created in case he ever catches up with Billy. I understand that by the fifth of September, his next birthday he can officially live away from home anyway. Now buzz off the pair of you we have work to do here." Once the police had left and there was a little gap in proceeding, Vanessa went through into the kitchen to give Billy a good big hug to see if he was ok. That turned out to be a huge mistake, because Billy burst into tears and sobbed his heart out. Once he'd had a good cry, more because of the kindness shown, than any new upset, Billy settled down again and got on with his work. He thought that it was a good job he had come to work because, as yet only a young lady called Judith had turned up, but she was a keen worker anyway.

Later that evening Billy went out to the counter for a chat with his boss. He said to her, "Boss, we seem to have a big problem. I appear to have cooked up too many mixed grilles and too much soup. 'Remember Old Mother Hubbard'. Well it's like that in here. The cold room is almost empty. I've even run out of sausages and bacon. There are still a few eggs and a little ham and a small amount of cheddar cheese but little of anything else. Then there is the pantry. It is almost as bad. We are even out of baked beans, there is very little bread and very little of anything else. Is there anywhere that we can get any bits of supplies to see us through the night."

"I can't get anything at this time on Sunday night. I planned for us to go shopping as soon as we knock off in the morning. How can we manage to get through until then, Have you got any special recipes up your sleeve that don't need any ingredients?"

"I never had a look in your pantry at the farm but if there is any stuff around that needs using up we could soon grab it. If Judith can drive your van she could take me home and we could raid the refrigerator and pantry cupboard and see what we can get. A quick look in the garden I might find some stuff to make soup, you know like carrots, parsnips, leeks, onions."

"Ok mate, away you go. Here are my keys. The biggest one fits the door we came out of around the back. You'll find a good lantern on the shelf outside the door so you can see in the garden. Don't take long I need you both here" said Vanessa.

Billy and Judith took off in a hurry. Judith said, "I hope you know what you're doing. I've never been to Vanessa's place, in fact I don't even know where it is so you'll have to navigate."

"Don't get too excited about that. I've only been there once and I was asleep on the way in anyway." Billy chipped in.

Most of the stock was only domestic sizes but there was some excess stock from the café stored in a large walk-in room next door to the pantry. They soon had a good load in the van. Fresh meat was a bit meagre but that would have to do. They raided the garden with a fair amount of success. There was some tinned corned beef and other similar stuff as well as a small quantity of cheese. Judith reversed the van up to the rear door of the café then helped Billy to carry the stock through the kitchen and into the store room and pantry. After a good wash up, especially his hands and Billy was back in business. Let's hope we don't get any coaches in tonight he said to Judith who had elected to prepare some food and meals under Billy's tutelage. As she stated, "It was no use being a waitress unless there was some food to serve and dishes to clear. So here I am awaiting your directions 'Oh' master chef." Billy grinned at Judith saying, "Things are starting to improve around here, yesterday was a total disaster."

"So I understand pal, I've heard a bit about it. I nearly didn't bother to come in today. I didn't know if we would be operating tonight, or ever again. Some of the stories I heard would make your hair stand on end."

Vanessa was as pleased as punch. Billy and Judith worked well together both in the kitchen and in the dining hall. By 6 o'clock the kitchen was sparkling again, all the dishes stacked away, both urns bubbling merrily away and the big kettle was on the boil again. One of the teapots was ready to serve tea that was brewing nicely, that meant the only problem was still a severe lack of ingredients. Billy turned to Vanessa saying, "After another bad start, everything settled down well, Boss, but please don't forget Judith, she was fantastic. Hard working, careful, and considerate as well. I couldn't have coped without her input. Teamwork, that's the name of our game. She is smart enough to know what is coming next instead of standing around waiting to be told what to do." Commented Billy.

Vanessa spoke to Billy. "Get your order pads mate we have some shopping to do. That was another great night's work you put in, thanks pal. If you can work like that every day you might have yourself a full time job. Being able to cook a decent meal at your age is quite an achievement mate and to be able to run and organise the kitchen and wait at table at the same time is fantastic. Come on hop in the van we have a lot to do before the day shift can start cooking again. We have standing orders with the butcher, the baker and the green grocer so they'll be able to do some preparation before we get back.

"Won't it be too early for the shops yet, Boss?" Billy asked Vanessa

"Yes for normal people but they serve trade outlets at the back door. It helps them and it helps us to get our stuff before they get busy. They deliver our set orders but if we need extra we come in the back door. So Mr Butcher, here we come. If we can get some of our needs we can run it straight back to the café.

Chapter Seven

"Now Michael, are you ready for business because we're in a hurry? Asked Vanessa, at the butchers shop.

"How are you today, Vanessa. I see you have a, helper. Who's this then? I don't think I ever seen this young man around here before." Asked Michael.

"This young man calls himself 'Billy the Kid." Replied Vanessa. "He is my new head chef. He's stirring hell out of my place, so look out, Michael here he comes."

"Bit young for a title like that, ain't he?" said Michael.

"Don't you worry about that Michael. He'll keep you on your toes. So let's get on. We are completely out of meat."

"Come on then chef, follow me. What do you need this morning? Asked Michael"

"A full string of your normal, thin sausages. Then, can you knock up a string of half length sausages. You can make them the same recipe as the big ones today if you like but from now on I want them made to this recipe. It's Italian style but you might have to get in some special herbs. Billy handed over a sheet of paper torn from the order book. Then we need a whole flitch of your best bacon. What have you got?

I select the best pigs from a nearby market then cure it myself. There's none of that factory bacon and ham here. Just have a look at this side, it just needs to be boned out and sliced."

"Ok, bone it out and slice it up if you please. We need it desperately"

"What, all of it Billy? That's a lot of bacon." Said Michael.

"You're right about that but we'll be trying a lot of new recipes including 'pizzas'. That's a sort of meat, cheese and tomato flan. I got the recipe from an Italian prisoner of war who was a qualified chef before being dragged into the army. Anyway, it'll keep in our cool room just as well as yours and I can rest assured that when I want some of it, I'll have the best quality available. I see you've already boned out a lot of meat this morning, can I buy all those bones please?" Billy queried. "Just run the bigger ones through the band saw to fit my pans and let the marrow out? We need one of the hams off that same bacon pig, if you still have it. You can bone it out so I can slice it but I want all the off-cuts including the bones. Right you are Michael now I need a lot of top quality mince meat. I don't want any fat and rubbish either. Then I need a heap of your best sausage meat to make into hamburgers and rissoles. Once you manage to get some of my recipe sausage meat I'll be needing lots of it loose, in bulk, as well as the half length sausages. Then we need some nice small loin chops for mixed grilles, cut them thin so they cook quick and don't weigh too much or they will be too expensive to use for mixed grilles. We'll be needing some small round, top quality steaks. Like the chops, nice and small, with very little fat and no sinews or gristle. We have to cook them quickly, but they still need to be tender, because travellers don't like to wait. That will do for now thanks Michael. "Can you put some of that together now please. We are going to annoy the baker now and will call back to get as much as is ready by then." "Yes, sir, Mr Chef, I'll do my best. Here's my apprentice he can get started on the sausages then bone and slice the bacon. Thanks for the big order to start the week off right. Once I get used to your ways and your recipes I'll be able to select and prepare some of it in advance"

Once they were back in the van, Billy turned to Vanessa saying, "I hope you have a healthy bank balance Boss. That was a big order but none of it will go to waste. Quite a lot of it will get used today. Was that Ok Boss?"

"I would have ordered at least half of that lot today anyway, seeing as you've robbed my pantry at home as well. Yes I was expecting that much but there were one or two surprises like all those bones, but you'll need them tonight to brew up for stock and soup. Well here we are, without a doubt the best baker for many miles. "Good morning Peter, how are you today? I hope you have plenty of bread ready for me."

"Yes of course Vanessa, is this the new chef that I'm hearing about?

"Peter, this is Billy the kid, the meanest chef in the town. Billy meet Peter our baker he'll look after all our needs and any special orders as well.

"So Vanessa what are you doing here shouldn't you be in bed by now? We are just putting your order together now. Are there some things extra that you need."

"Just put the regular order in my van please, Peter, whilst Billy has a look around. He's bound to want more for some of his special menus. Things are changing big time from today. Billy will want to ask you about special breads and something called pizza dough and pizza bases. They are Italian apparently. We ran out of bread and rolls and everything last night so I have delegated Billy to do all the ordering from now on, It will probably take him a week or two to settle in then 'look out' Haversby." By the time Billy had seen everything he needed for now the van was loaded ready for a quick run to back to the butcher's then back to the café.

Billy was unloading the goodies whilst explaining to the day cook, Jennifer, what he expected of her until he had everything sorted out. The menus needed a complete overhaul even without Billy's new ideas and recipes. He asked her to get some of the best bones cooking ready for the vegetables when they arrived. Vanessa had organised mugs of tea for themselves, then it was back on the road.

The next stop was to the green grocer, Ernie, who was a big jovial man with a quick wit and a colossal smile. When introduced to Billy he shook his hand stating, "Nice to meet you Billy. So you're going to straighten out our Vanessa and that tin-pot café of hers and about time too. That roadhouse should be a great little goldmine if it's run properly. Of course, you can't expect a woman, not even one as cute as Vanessa to organise and run a big set up like that. It needs a good strong minded man to pull it all together. Although you might be a bit on the young side I can see how determined you are and you can rest assured that the traders like me, and Michael and Peter will help all we can. We're very open minded and this 'two-bob' town needs some new blood and new ideas to fire it up. If the road house picks up trade, as I'm sure it will, it means that our businesses will improve along with it. So that's all the twaddle out of the way, what can I do for you today?

Billy couldn't help a little grin to himself. Here was another great character and he was looking forward to working with him and the others. A little bit of banter and camaraderie helps to lighten the atmosphere making working together much smoother. "Ok then for a start I'm starting new menus such as a variety of soups, stews and casseroles as well as curries. That means more quality root vegetables on top of our current order. One point I should make is that at the end of each week I will be able to use a few slightly stale roots for the soups so long as they are still sound. This should help you to clear your shelves towards the end of the week so that you start fresh on Mondays. So long as the price is suitably adjusted I should be able to help you and greatly reduce my input costs at the same time".

"I like the sound of most of that young man except the last bit. I can see there will a certain amount of discounting going on but the word 'greatly' worries me a bit."

"That was only a figure of speech Ernie, not

serious but I'm sure you can see my meaning." Billy replied.

"Ok then young man let's shake on that and see how it all pans out. Do you require anything extra to your regular order this morning? The boys are putting it up now then we'll deliver it shortly."

"We are brewing up some soups and stews etc right about now so I was thinking about maybe parsnips, carrots, Swedes, leeks, turnips and celery."

"Why don't we go out to the back pal to see what the boys have put aside to go out before they dump it. Maybe you can use some of it and it's free today if you want any of it." Replied Ernie. He and Billy did just that and there was a good quantity that they salvaged. "That's great mate now we can see what's required the lads can put it aside. How about half price for a start then we will see how it goes."

The co-op super-market was visited next to organise more herbs and spices. Then Billy was expecting to go home to bed. He was absolutely knackered but his Boss was not quite finished with him yet. There was a clothing store and general outfitter at the end of the main street shopping area. Vanessa parked around by the rear door, shouted out and entered into a vestibule area. "She called out Muriel are you about or shall we just help ourselves?"

A slightly overweight but very elegant, lady appeared from out of a storeroom, she retorted, "So what's all the noise about. Is there a fire somewhere? Oh it's only you Vanessa and this must be your new fancy-man. Hello young man do you have a fancy name, then."

"Aye well yes but it's a bit unusual. My surname is Cheeky. "That made Vanessa's ears pop up, She was hoping to solve the next saga in the puzzle of who Billy was and where he came from, but only for a second. When Muriel asked, "What about a first name. Do you have one of them an' all."

"Yes of course, madam, "Its, Ayedontbe."

"Ayedontbe? What sort of a name is that? It must be Irish, is it?

"Nay Mrs. It's North of England, Ayedontbe. My full handle is 'Ayedontbe Cheeky' in good proper English."

"My god Vanessa what the hell have you

found here? We'll all have to watch our 'P's and 'Q's from now on. Have you just come around to annoy hell out of me, or are you just showing off your fancy man." Quite formally now Vanessa stretched up to her full height before saying, "That's enough of your smart arsed remarks madam. We can soon go to the other outfitter's shop in town you know. This young gentleman is my new "Chef" Billy the kid. As suits his new position in an upper class restaurant, he needs to be outfitted in the best apparel available from your meagre store. I realise you might not come up to our high ideals, in which case we'll have to seek quality elsewhere.

"In that case you had better bring him through here. We are bound to have something to suit the young gentleman. Come along Billy."

"Billy has virtually nothing to speak of so let's start with underwear, socks, jocks and Vests. Then shirts, tee shirts, tops. He will need lightweight cotton type trousers and shorts suitable for hot kitchens. Lightweight jackets, all in matching styles and colours." Stated Vanessa.

Hazel Watkins would be happy to run up

some nice classy threads for our Chef here."

"Billy arrived with only little more than rags and not too much of that either so he wants to buy some good stuff for street wear as well as his uniforms. Maybe if you kit him out with basic underwear for today then we can go out to your rear emporium, tomorrow, there are probably some good used or near new articles in that assortment to fit him." Remarked Vanessa.

"Seriously, that's very true, I had a large shipment come in last week. They must have come from a classy suburb or town. The old lady what owned the shop had a heart attack and passed away apparently so when I was offered the whole job lot by the estate agent so that he could clear the building, I grabbed it. I haven't had time to sort it through yet but if you have time today you can go through it with me."

"Make that tomorrow we've been on all night. We need a good shower then a few hours sleep. We're not back on duty again until Thursday night then so we'll have plenty of time then. Take Billy's measurements now and talk to Hazel if you would, see what time she has available. In the meantime if you have the time to spend you could sort out a good range in Billy's sizes and put them aside. That will save time later. Billy will need two of everything and three sets of underwear. Hazel may find something in all this rubbish that you stock that she can alter to get a better fit for him. I want him to look like a well bred gentleman when he escorts me around Cheltenham and places like that. Don't worry too much about fancy evening wear. We won't be going to the opera this season."

"Out! Get out! Before I chuck you out, madam, you're cheekier than Billy is and that's saying summat. Go and make some tea and toast see if you can poison someone. Bye Vanessa, Bye Billy, see you both in a day or two."

"When they were in the van, Billy asked Vanessa, a serious question. "I'm nearly skint how can I afford all that Vanessa? I know I desperately need it but it'll cost lots of money. May be I should wait awhile until I get a few bob in the bank. I don't want to be in debt, owing money to you and Muriel as well."

"No, no, Billy Muriel will be very kind to you, She likes you even though you are a cheeky little monkey. She'll be very reasonable. She really enjoyed that little wrangle with you today. It tickled her taste buds and whetted her appetite for more of the same next time. That big consignment that she told us about she would have got for next to nothing. Probably only for the cartage to get it here. She's a cunning old rat but she has a heart of gold. Let's just see what she comes up with. I'll have to outfit you for work and the street wear won't break the bank. You probably spent more of my money in the butcher's shop this morning.

Once they were back at the farm Billy watched as Vanessa attended to the AGA cooking stove, It had a water element in the rear flue so there would always be plenty of hot showers or baths. Billy had never seen a shower before let alone indulged in the luxury of steaming hot water pouring over his body and soothing his wounds. This must be close to heaven. At home there was also plenty of hot water from a boiler behind the kitchen fire and the cottage was connected to the main water supply but he was only allowed a bath once a week and then it was in his sister's used bath water. Once he was well soaked and dry Vanessa checked all his sores and she was well pleased with the results of her ministrations. She dressed them all again before dosing the whole area with healing liniment. He was ready for his bed and was asleep before Vanessa could offer him tea and biscuits. He slept for the rest of the day before awakening about 5.30. pm. He could hear Vanessa down stairs. She appeared to be very annoyed about something so he pulled on some clothes and went down stairs quickly. Vanessa was strutting around in the kitchen fuming mad. "What's happened Vanessa, Billy asked? Why are you so upset? Can I do anything to help?"

"I just wish there were two of you Billy or maybe three or four, then you could run and manage the kitchen round the clock."

"You haven't met Elizabeth yet. She just sent a message to say that she was knocked off her bike this afternoon. She is in Cheltenham hospital with a broken arm and leg. She will be off work for weeks. It wasn't her fault. A motor-cyclist ran her into the ditch. He's worse than Elizabeth. Serves the beggar right. That means I need a cook for tonight, for starters. Then I'll need someone for three nights per week for the next six weeks or so. What can I do? I've used up all my reserves this weekend so now there's no one to help me out. I'll have to close the kitchen for the night then see who I can dig up for the rest of the week."

"Hey Boss slow down. I'll go in, now, cook and manage the kitchen for tonight. That will give you a breathing space. I'm quite happy to fill in for the rest of the week then work with you next weekend. Hopefully by then you'll have sorted something out."

"No Billy, don't be stupid. You need to rest up for next weekend. I can't expect you to carry on by yourself."

"You can and you will. Remember, I only worked two nights this weekend, you worked 4 nights so I can work 4 nights straight. Apart from anything else, I need to earn extra to pay for my clothes. I still need shoes and boots too. They will have to be new ones. A pair of Wellingtons might be needed as well."

"God you're a stubborn bugger Billy. Ok, you can do it, but you've got to promise me faithfully that you will knock off and come home if it gets too much for you to manage.

"Right you are Boss. I'll pop upstairs and finish dressing then you can deliver me into the lion's den in your chariot."

Monday nights were never really busy. There were plenty of lorries but the drivers were not pushy like car drivers so Billy and Jennifer enjoyed their company. Most of the lorry drivers wanted a break as well as a meal so they were happy to wait and chat with other drivers. Long distance lorry driving is a very lonely job. There were no two-way radios in those days, only a few upmarket cars were fitted with radios at all. During the 12 hour shift, Billy had enough time to organise the cool room and the pantry stocks. He also moved some of the crockery and cutlery around to make life a lot easier for everyone. Just a little before 6am Vanessa arrived to take him home for a hot shower and redressing of his back and bottom. As she expected the kitchen was all nice and clean and shiny with no dirty pots and pans around. There were large pots of homemade soups and meaty stews ready to go. Billy greeted Vanessa saying, "Hey Boss I need your taste buds for one of my recipes.

I had a crack at making a mutton curry with some of that cheaper meat I got from Michael. I found a recipe in an Indian cooking book that he gave me. Please have a taste see what you think." He put a generous portion of the curry onto a dish and handed it to her. Vanessa had tasted curry before and really liked the taste but she was very cautious of this one in case it was too 'hot' or spicy. It takes a lot of practice to get the taste and spices in balance but Billy had cracked it quite well. There was still plenty of room to experiment and there were many different tastes to suit various palates. However, the Boss enjoyed Billy's first attempt. She came back for seconds because she had not eaten as yet and this would do for her breakfast she said. The café now had a good range of meals that were much cheaper to provide with a better profit margin, so the girls had written up a blackboard menu near the counter entitled <u>TODAYS SPECIALS.</u> The other advantage of these meal types was that they could be ready to serve or at least only needing a quick reheating. Many travellers would surely find this a great help and good nutritious meals could be devoured quickly to save them time. A good dollop of mashed spuds or boiled rice rounded them off into a good, solid meal.

"Come on Billy, time to go shopping again. What have you got on your list today more meat or what?"

"Not much Boss, baker's first to update our order. I need to have a chat with Peter about base dough for my pizza recipe but that is not urgent. I do need to see the butcher about some cheaper cuts of mutton and beef suitable for the curry, stews and casseroles. We can make a lot of extra money with those cheaper meals. Gourmet meals are good for those people who can afford them but we need to feed the masses with good grub. Then we have to go to the co-op and search through their herbs and spices. We may have to arrange for them to order in more and different spices for the curries and casseroles."

"Right you are then, the butcher, the baker's then the Co-op shop." replied Vanessa.

With the food shopping out of the way Vanessa returned to the clothing emporium to see if Muriel had come up with lots of goodies.

As they walked in through the rear door again Muriel called out, "I'm glad you came around today I have heaps to show you and Hazel reckoned she would be here soon. The sooner she meets Billy the better to sort him out. I've got three full sets of underwear and socks put aside in that box so you can take that out to the van now. They should all fit but I can change any of them if you are not happy with the styles or fit. 'Ere 'ave a look at this Billy boy, it will suit you well, It'll make you look real posh, She was holding up a dark blue, clip-on, bow tie. With this on your shirt you'll look like a real chef."

"You have been busy Muriel? Did you get chance to look through the other lot from Bristol?" Vanessa asked.

"Yes and no. They have been shipped, as was, so to speak. There are many racks of girls and ladies wear still on their original racks and hangers. Also, I found lots of men's wear on racks. Much of the small stuff has been folded into boxes so it is much harder to find out what's in there. I have found quite a lot of street clothing though, about the right size, and boxes of pyjamas and shirts. There is one box loaded with 'T' shirts. This is Hazel coming in the front door now so we can make a start. I'll just introduce you then I have to serve in the shop so I'll leave you with Hazel. In here Hazel come through and meet Vanessa and Billy. After greeting each other Vanessa said to Hazel, "Sorry about this Hazel, Billy has been working all through the night because Elizabeth had an accident and she's in hospital. He needs to get home soon get a shower and as much sleep as he can. I'll come straight back and help you go through some of this lot. We can have a fitting session early tomorrow morning if that suits you."

"Yes that'll be fine. I can work through this and then Muriel will have a better idea of what she has here. These are beautiful clothes Vanessa. Some look brand new, never been worn. It looks like they've all been carefully laundered or dry-cleaned. I doubt we'll find any work clothes though. We may have to start from scratch or maybe order some basic stuff in and alter if necessary. Leave it with me and we'll see you in the morning. Is Billy likely to be working tonight as well?"

"I don't want him to work but with Elizabeth incapacitated he might have to but we'll see. Bye, then and have fun."

"Well young man how are you feeling about all those lovely clothes now? You'll look a real gentleman by the time Hazel and Muriel finish with you. I'll have to keep you locked up from now on to make sure the local lasses don't abduct you." Said Vanessa with a grin.

"Can we call into the roadhouse as we go passed in case Jennifer has any problems with the new menus." Billy asked.

"Might as well, we go right passed, but I don't want you hanging around. It's shower and bed for you my boy with maybe a cup of tea and a cream bun"

All was well in the kitchen. Jennifer was shaping up well. She at least would work in well with the new menus and recipes. Vanessa drove out to the farm and soon had Billy tucked up in his bed. When he awoke again it was almost time to dress and go to work. This was good for him as he had no time to dwell on the past. After another successful nights work Vanessa was waiting to take Billy home after a quick look into the clothing shop. Once there he tried on a number of articles of clothing, which proved to be ok. Hazel came in as they were about to leave. Good morning young man come through I have some outfits to show you that I can adjust if necessary to get a really good fit. I found three pairs of cotton trousers that should fit you and look real hot. Then I came across these sky blue long sleeved cotton shirts, which match up nicely with the trousers. That should set you up for working in the kitchen. What do you think about that for hick shop?"

"Gosh Hazel, they'll look very professional on me. I'll look like a real chef in those. What do you reckon Boss, will they do me?"

"Only if you wear the blue bow-tie, Billy." Vanessa replied." Stick them on quick then we can get going". If they fit well, you can wear one set tonight. Those old things you have on are just about to fall off you. You look a bit like a scarecrow."

The outfits fitted nicely with a little bit of

spare room to accommodate a quickly filling out of Billy's belly and other bits. He was already showing signs of reaction to all the good food. They called in at the café and had a quick word with Jennifer then home to the shower to remove the smell and detritus of his night's work.

Vanessa was getting a bit despondent about staff vacancies. She'd put adverts in the local papers and expected some replies by now but it appeared that there were no cooks or chefs available at the moment. Billy had suggested that she advertise for waitresses and/or kitchen hands specifying, either male or female. That way they might at least get someone to assist Billy at night. By the time they arrived home the local paper had arrived showing the adverts. Vanessa had listed the home phone number so she could interview potential candidates without interruptions. Billy jumped into the shower first. When he was dressed he hurried back down stairs and accosted Vanessa. "Billy asked Where can I find a newsagent around here Boss, Is there one close by?

"Yes there's a newsagent and book shop.

Just turn right after the clothing store, you can't miss it. What do you want from a book-shop Mate? I've got heaps of books in the library. Come here I'll give you a bit of a grand tour so you can find things when you want them." She led Billy into a long hallway on the ground floor. The last door on the right was a spacious library well filled with books. "Any time you need something to read just come in and help yourself. This is a magic room. I often come in here for a bit of peace and quiet."

The French Doors opened on to the patio and gardens as well as a good view of the bend in the river Avon. This was the sunny side of the house. Billy said, "No boss, what I need is a few magazines. All the latest cooking ideas, and recipes. I had quite a few at home but I had to leave them behind. I kept them hidden in my room so my old man wouldn't see them and rib shit out of me for reading sissy books. There are a few that specialise on food and cooking and then, there are the women's magazines, some of them feature food and recipes.

I'd like to get some of the gourmet and epicure magazines but the good ones cost a fair bit. When I manage to get some wages out of my tight old boss I'd like to stock up my library again."

"Hey, enough of the insults! When you've done a fair bit of work I might pay you a bob or two but in the meantime hop on your bike and go down there see what they have. I have a shop account with them for the daily papers and magazines that we sell in the café, just ask Penny to put them on my account. If you need any real specials she might have to order them in for you. Hey you young Billy, now I've got it. I've been wondering where all these menus and recipes were coming from, so that's it, magazines. Well you must have a fantastic memory."

"Ok caught out again, do I get punished for my sins?"

"Hardly sins mate. I just wondered where it all came from. Most lads of your age can't even boil water or make a cup of tea. When did all this begin Billy?"

"A girl in my class at the grammar school lived with her parents who owned a fancy café on the A1 road near our place. She had moved from another area and was well behind and struggling with mathematics, Latin and French so I used to hop off the bus at her place weekdays and we studied together. I started riding my bike up there on the weekends whenever Dad didn't need me. I practically lived there most weekends. Charlotte's grades soon jumped up and she caught up with the rest of us. Her grades went up from the lower 10 % in class to the top 10% in two terms. I had a great opportunity to observe her mother and father in their kitchen and I helped out as much as I could especially when they had large gatherings and tourist coaches often called in for a meal stop. Quite a bit of it stuck, obviously so here I am. Dad would have gone mad and belted all that stupidity out of me. He was determined that I would become a mechanic or some sort of engineer."

"Surely not, Billy. You have a natural flare for cooking and cuisine. He wouldn't take that away from you, mate, would he?"

"He certainly would. No son of his was going to be a woozy cook or chef. I barely mentioned it one day after I had spent the day at 'White

Gables' with Charlotte and her family and the old man nearly knocked my block off.

"Ok pal, get away down to the news agents and hurry back then bed.

"Gee whiz boss that's great I'll see you soon. Where did you hide my bike?"

"It's in the second loose box at this side of the yard." Billy was off, lickety-split, out of the door before Vanessa called him back to finish dressing properly and put on a coat. Billy spent a while scouring the shelves and store room at the news agency. There he discovered a couple of current issues of Gourmet Cooking magazine that he wanted but in the store room there were a couple more out of date but unsold copies which he received for half price. He asked the store to supply him with each monthly edition until notified to stop. He was over the moon and couldn't get back quick enough to show them off to Vanessa. His boss however, although pleased for him, took them off him and sent him straight to bed. Gourmet Cooking indeed, it would have to wait until he had caught up with the much needed gourmet sleep.

There was still a twelve-hour shift to cope

with that night. Whenever the café was a bit quiet, Billy spent any spare time he could grab trying out recipes to add to the menu boards. In one of the back issues of Gourmet Cooking he found a recipe and instructions for making burgers American style. He would have to get Peter to bake some special bread buns to suit. He needed to have large flat buns with lots of sesame seeds on the top. Peter was quite willing to provide them for him and ended up selling them to householders and pubs as well to go with the new craze called 'Barbeque cooking.' Billy lightly toasted the cut side of the buns before filling them with a meat patty made from the special sausage meat from Michael with secretly added herbs and spices from the co-op. He tried the burgers out on the staff at first then some local people before putting them on the menu board for the general public. The burgers were a great success with everyone. The lorry drivers particularly enjoyed the new menus. They were sick of the same old sandwiches and mixed grilles. As time went by Billy would add extra ingredients to spice up the burgers. Like sliced, cheese, eggs, and bacon. The burgers went well as a main meal, served with crispy, deep fried chips, as an addition to one of his soups or casseroles. One piece of good news came to hand that day, kitchen hands were around and available, and some of them were willing to learn about cooking, to become competent cooks, lack of which was a problem in the town.

Chapter Eight

Billy had been so well occupied that he hadn't given a thought to what was happening back in his old home and any way, why should he care? His mother and Maude were copping the worst of the flak. Did Billy care? Not even a little bit. All the people around the roadhouse, loved, admired and respected him, although it was still early days. It was hard to appreciate that it had been only a little over one week since his escape into this new world. Meanwhile poor Maude was copping all the extra work at 'home'. She was made to take on all Billy's old chores on top of everything else. The favourite retort from Ethel and to a lesser extent from Joe was, "Our Billy managed to do it all on top of his home work so you can do it now. You never lifted a finger to help him. He had to work with his dad felling trees and cutting them into logs and kindling wood every weekend. He often came home with a crop of blisters on his hands and a few cuts and bruises as well. Remember our Billy went out night after night to collect sugar beet, cut and boil some of it up, and trail it down to the orchard to feed the pigs. All you could do was to fret about going to the bloody youth club."

"Now he's gone it'll make you realise how well off you were before, so keep your gob shut or I'll shut it for you," said Ethel. "You've been nothing but a spoilt brat all your life. I've had to do extra housework because you wouldn't help me. I'm working full time in the bullet factory now and with a long ride morning and night in all sorts of weather, yet when I get home at night I have to light the fire then start tea and wash up afterwards while you sit on your arse reading comics. Well I can tell you young lady, from now on the tea had better be ready on the table when I walk in or you'll feel the big wooden spoon across your arse"

"If you did hit me my dad would soon sort you out, so there our mum." Ethel moved close to Maude and smacked her across the face, "Well start with that young lady."

"Dad would be more likely to put his belt around you if you upset me. I had a long talk with him last night and he agrees with me. If we are going to get through this mess we will all have to pitch in and share the load. Dad and I work long hard hours on our feet all day. Then I have to cycle all the way to and from Fransby. It takes a long while to get home. I am usually nithered [very cold] by the time I get in and it'll be worse now that winter is settling in. I get home only to find that I have to get some kindling and get a fire going to cook our dinner on. Then, what do I find, you sitting around on your arse whinging about how badly you're treated. From now on young lady the fire is your responsibility. Hot water, hot oven, warm house by the time I get home. The table has to be set and veges peeled and cooking in the pot. Also starting now you do all your own laundry and ironing." Anyway, if you want to give it a go and push your luck do it now. I'll go and get the wooden spoon, and I'll probably break it on your arse before I finish with it tonight."

Maude realise that her mum really meant what she was saying so she jumped up quickly and started to set the table for tea. Complaining as she did so, "Why should I have to do it. I never had to before it was always our Billy's job. Some of it is too hard for me. The coal bucket is far too heavy for me to carry. I'm not strong like our Billy."

"Fill the bloody bucket half way you silly bitch and if you mention our Billy again you will get that wooden spoon and maybe dad's belt as well when I tell him you are refusing to help me."

"I'm not refusing to help just pointing out that I aren't very strong. I've had a hard day at school, don't you know?"

Ethel had had enough she picked up the wooden spoon and waved it in Maude's face, saying, "Do you want a taste of this now?" Apparently Maude didn't as she shot outside to get some logs for the fire. When Joe came home for tea he announced, "As soon as I get finished in t'morning we'll have us our bit of dinner then get away to Boston and see if Mum or our Emily have heard anything of our Billy. If they haven't we'll double back into Barrestown to have another talk with the Skotchdales. Maybe Tony will have been contacted and have some idea where to look next. If we don't find him tomorrow we'll 'ave to get up early on Sunday morning and go up to Durham.

"All this is a pain in the bloody arse. What the hell does he think he's doing? Think about all I've done for that rotten bugger over the last 14 years and now he's just getting useful for me he buggers off. How am I ever going to get any work done around here? Hey! Our lass you'll 'ave to collect some sugar beet every night as soon as you get home from school."

"I can't balance my bike with big bags of sugar beet on the handle bars and anyway you don't let me ride on the main road on my own so you'll have to come with me."

If that rotten bugger has headed to Durham, he'll have gotten to your Nelson's by Sunday. We might be able to get a free load of coal to bring back if Nelson has had a delivery recently. That'll help with the petrol expenses. I'd better remember to chuck in a few potato sacks just in case. On the way home if we don't find him at Nelson's place we'll drop into your Terence just in case he's arrived there. We can just as easily come home down the A1 instead of the A19.

During a quick trip to Boston Spa, Joe gave his mother and his sister a hard time because he reckoned they might be hiding Billy. They went straight to Barrestown from Boston Spa as they had done the week before but the Skotchdales declared that they had seen neither hide nor hair of him. Joe got stuck into Tony because he was sure that, he at least, would have heard something by now. Herbert Stockdale shouted at Joe to leave Tony alone, unless he wanted his head knocked off. Then pushed them out of the door and locked it behind them.

First thing Sunday morning Joe fed the pigs very early so they could leave straight after breakfast. It was still quite early as they turned onto the A19 highway but the weather appeared settled so they could enjoy the 60 mile journey through Thirsk, and Yarm. They arrived at Nelson's place mid morning much to Doris's surprise. The coal fire was always burning and the kettle pushed to one side where it was always on the boil. Doris welcomed them in but pointed out that Nelson was working on his allotment, but would maybe, arrive home shortly. Most of the miners leased small plots of garden mainly to grow vegetables. Some kept a few hens and some even racing pigeons

When Nelson arrived he was keen to know why Ethel and Joe were there on this particular day. Joe told them the gist of the story about Billy but omitting the more violent parts. Nelson smelled a rat and in the cross fire Maude let slip the main thrust of the problem. Nelson was a hard man himself and ruled his household and family with an iron fist but he was appalled that poor Billy had been so badly treated that he left home. Nelson gave out a savage growl telling Joe to get out of his home and never come back again. He was very close to giving Joe a good hiding as well. He told Joe and Ethel, "If our Billy does show up here he will be welcomed with open arms. Now that two of our girls are away and living in at Sedgefield Hospital, where they are training to be nurses, there is a spare room here for Billy if he wants it and I will fight you to the end for the right to love and protect him, so get your arses out of our home now right now."

Ethel was devastated. Her mother had died quite young leaving behind a long brood of kids. Being the oldest girl in a family of 10 she had been mother to all the others. Her father had dragged her out of school when she could barely write her name. She had fed them, bathed them, clothed them and nearly starved herself to death to feed them all whilst her father drank most of his wages in the miner's club. Ethel often said that, had it not been for Salvation Army soup kitchens they would all have starved to death.

Joe bundled his family out of the house and back into the car. Ethel was in tears. She was sobbing her heart out. Joe yelled at her, "For God's sake woman, shut your bloody noise. It won't help us to listen to that racket all the way home nor will it help us find our Billy." Joe drove off without another word except to lament the fact that they were forced to leave without getting a few bags of coal. That fact seemed to be upsetting him far more than not finding Billy, and getting his backside kicked out of Nelson's home meant that the free coal supply would be a thing of the past.

Ethel had always thought of Nelson as her favourite brother and he was the only family member that she ever wanted to visit. She had a sister in Cowley but distance made visiting her difficult. They drove over to Berrytown near the A1, to Terence's home. Terence was her second eldest brother after their Jack and they would have to treat him with caution lest they received the same treatment as they received at Nelson's place. Joe gave Maude a severe talking to, telling her to keep her big gob shut and let him do all the talking.

After effusive greetings and cups of tea, Joe asked Terence and Kristy if they knew the whereabouts of Billy. He only mentioned that Billy had become unsettled at school and around home before deciding to run away on a camping trip. He suggested that the boy would soon get over his dummy spit and return home before the next school term began. As Joe suggested, it was one thing running away in the warm summer days and sleeping out under a hedge but come the first frosty nights he would soon scramble back to his nice warm bed. It soon became obvious that Terence and Kristy had no knowledge of Billy's whereabouts so Joe bundled everyone back into the car and headed for home. They stopped at a couple of wayside cafés along the A1 Highway where lorries often stopped for fuel and meals. Joe described Billy's unusual bicycle rig-out but there had been no sightings of his outfit. Joe had a bit of an idea so he said to his wife, "Look here Ethel, our Billy has to be somewhere around. Maybe we're looking in wrong direction. In't' morning why don't you drop a line to your Marion in Cowley, see if he went that way?"

Chapter Nine

Meanwhile, back at the roadhouse things had settled down quite nicely in spite of the lack of night cooks. Once the new staff had settled in Billy still needed to assist with the night cooking seven days per week. The new menus and recipes meant that many of the meals could be served by the wait staff and kitchen hands. They didn't really need a qualified cook or chef. Many of the new menus needed only commonsense and diligence. The kitchen should be able to operate just as efficiently as if he was there. Billy only needed to turn up at the café at 6am and 6.pm every day to advise the incoming shift. He worked through until the nights menus and main meals had been attended to then he was able to leave the kitchen to others and sneak off home to bed. Most nights by about midnight Billy was happy to leave the job to the kitchen hands. It mostly consisted of reheating the soups or stews, even the curry and casseroles were very easy to reheat and serve, along with generous portions of crusty bread or toast. Of course the teapot was always on hand and anyone could keep refilling the hot water urns. Standard roadhouse meals such as mixed grills, scrambled eggs, and bacon and eggs were well within the capacity of the kitchen hands. Both of the night time kitchen hands were keen to learn all the tricks of the trade and become competent cooks or ultimately chefs and there was no better place than a busy roadside café to do that. All members of the staff were responsible for cleanliness both in the kitchen and out in the dining room. Billy had instilled into each member of staff that it was their responsibility to attend to any spills or mess that they noticed. He told them that it's not some other person's job or responsibility to keep the café spotless at all times.

On the Monday evening Billy dressed up in his new finery. The dark blue trousers fitted well as did the long sleeved shirt. He really felt like a real chef now. He was about to leave for work when he remembered the dark blue bow tie that Muriel had found. It was still lying in the underwear box so he fished it out and snapped it on to his shirt collars, which he now needed to wear with the top button fastened. Looking at himself in the full-length mirror in Vanessa's bedroom he called out. "Oh my God, cop this. Mr. Chef here I come. He was amazed at the difference something so small could make. When he entered the café, there many shouts and cat-calls from his work mates and the few customers who were present. They all congratulated him and told him how smart he looked. Some of them asked if the food would be any better now that he was dressed for the part. Billy took it all in with good humour and a huge smile. He even looked a couple of years older as he held himself proudly erect. Once all the fun and frivolity had settled down Billy clapped his hands and called his helpers to the battle-front. He carried out a thorough inspection of the premises and tools then he took out the order book before checking right through the pantry, store cupboard, and cold store. The big cooking pots were on the stove primed with goodies and slowly cooking away. He picked up a spoon and gave them each a taste test. Maybe a touch more seasoning here and a little extra spice over there but otherwise all was well. Billy and Vanessa were amazed at how much easier everything went provided each shift cared for the next one.

Monday night was always quite busy because all the lorry drivers were back on the road after a weekend with their families. Already some of the drivers were making comments about the reports that they had heard of from other drivers concerning the new menus and the quick meals. Home away from home was the catch word now. The new instant menus greatly reduce the pressure of feeding a lot of people quickly. Billy had a good deal of help with the butcher and the green grocer. There was always a fair amount of good rivalry and camaraderie between them whenever they met up which pleased Billy. It made him feel good almost like an adult in fact and Michael, Peter, and Eric treated him as an adult. They respected this thoughts and ideas for new ways of pleasing the customers as well reducing waste and making more money. One thing Vanessa noticed was the steady increase of locals heading this way for evening meals instead of cooking at home. With more people dining in the café the atmosphere improved greatly.

One day a travelling salesman called in for a quick lunch and he was amazed at the range and type of meals now on offer. Once he had eaten his fill he asked to see the Boss. Mary was on the till and after taking his money for the meal she stuck her head through the hatch and yelled for Billy who was still in the kitchen fortunately. When Billy came through Mary said, "Here you are Billy you can be Boss today. This bloke is a sales representative for some mob as sells packaging stuff. I have far too much on today to waste time talking to travellers."

Turning back to the sales rep. She said, "This is Billy our chef. Show 'im what you 'ave then bugger off out of our way."

"Let's find an empty table in a corner somewhere where we can talk. Don't worry about Mary, she's in one of her moods again today but her barks worse than her bite. Do you have a business card so I can see who you are. Who are you anyway? What company do you represent?" Asked Billy.

The card that George presented told the story. They shook hands and got down to business. Billy said, "I'm looking into take away meals for the customers who are in a hurry. We'll need take away drink containers with lids, wrappers or fold away boxes for burgers and containers with lids to hold stews and curries like the Chinese restaurants use on the television. The drink containers have to be top of the range to minimise tainting and taste. I heard there is a good selection of plastic trays and dishes to hold hot food and they need to have lids. I'm not familiar with the takeaway side of things because I grew up on a farm miles from anywhere, right out in the countryside. I have never actually seen a Chinese or Indian restaurant only seen them on television shows, so I'll have to trust you to do the right thing by me, however, I do have quite a lot of recipes in that style and will soon get more."

"Ok, we can supply all of those for you and

all top quality. I'll just pop out to my car to get some catalogues and order pads and samples. You'll probably need some plastic carry bags because family groups and party hosts will want to take a mixed selection to feed their guests. I would suggest that at certain times like weekends you'll need to expand the range to take in a range of stir-fry recipes as well and even fish and chips." Said George. He brought in a selection of catalogues and they worked through them and ordered a selection. George was about to leave when he remembered a couple of menu samples in his briefcase. Pulling them out he gave them to Billy. One was a card for a Chinese Takeaway restaurant and the other was for an Indian Takeaway restaurant. George shook hands with Billy before saying "Thank you for your order Billy it was so unexpected. I'll forget to pick up those Asian menus. If you find them you won't remember where they came from, will you? You might even need to cut the headings off the top before anyone sees them. If you need further supplies before I call again just fill out one of those order forms and mail it back to us.

"Thank you George, if I manage to pull this off it will mean more business for you as well as us. How soon can you get some of this to us, say maybe overnight. It will be quite a job rearranging the store room to set them out. I am cook from 6 pm on Friday, Saturday and Sunday nights so I might come in a bit earlier to do some preparation, play around with recipes and see what happens. If we have your containers on hand, say early Friday morning we can run it as a weekend special starting this Friday evening, to judge the reactions. Do your firm deliver to us or will we be relying on couriers. I can't wait 'til this weekend to get started but I, and my staff will experimenting all week. Every spare moment is precious now until I get all this to the point that most of it will run itself. I can't and don't intend to be here all the time so I have to bring any new recruits along with me. Hopefully they or at least some of them will come up to scratch quite quickly and those that don't will have to find a handy space in the nearby dole queue"

"Delivery is very important Billy. Good job you thought of that, but you don't need to worry you are close enough for us to deliver so long as it is a decent order. If you need small deliveries we just use the post office parcels service. It's by far the cheapest and quickest. They deliver overnight mostly."

"Right you are then George we'll look forward to your next visit in about a month you say. By then we'll have a better idea where we are heading." Said William, "Bye now and thanks again."

George said, "Goodbye Billy, I hope you have a lot of fun with all this."

The immediate impact of George's visit was a big rearrangement and upheaval and in the storeroom to, hopefully, fit all the order on the shelves.

The packaging factory excelled Billy's best expectations. George had obviously hurried them up because mid-morning the very next day a large delivery van pulled in around the back of the kitchen ready to unload The driver apologised for some shortages but the boss had sent most of the stock ordered except for some items that would be scheduled for urgent production. They would then be delivered as soon as they had been manufactured. He promised to telephone Billy just prior to loading in case he wished to add to the order. The kitchen staff helped the driver to carry in the packaging and store it away for now. Billy now needed to work out which items he could use straight away and have them on hand. Meanwhile the menu boards would have to be upgraded to advertise the new lines. This was going to be another very hectic day. Billy thought that he was up to it, but would the rest of the crew cope. Time alone would answer that one and the new crew members were very willing to try.

Chapter Ten

Maude was dreading another weekend. Her dad was getting worse each week. He was quite alright during the week when he had his job to keep his mind occupied but as soon as his work was done on Saturday lunch time he went berserk. She realised that unless she was very careful she would cop the full force of his anger and she had seen what that did to Billy. This week she spoke to her mother mid week. She asked if it would be ok to sleep over at her friend Dora's home, which she was prone to do on a regular basis. Instead of coming home on the Friday night after school she would go straight to Dora's home with her friend and only return back home here on the Monday night because there were no buses at the weekend. Her mum wasn't happy about that as it would mean a lot more work for her. In the end she told Maude that she had to get ahead with the household chores like stripping and changing the bed linen, laundry and ironing, by Thursday night then she could go. Ethel knew Maude was scared stiff of what Joe might do to her when he lost his temper so she said, "Look Maude, just keep this to ourselves, don't mention it to Dad. Take your weekend case to school with you then off you go. If we end up charging around again this weekend there won't be too much to do around here anyway so I should be able to manage. Oh! How I wish our Billy were here. I miss him so much. It's only now he's not here that I realise just how much work he did around the place. I never had to ask him to do any of it. He just got on and did it all so we never realised that it had been done or even needed to be done. I do hope he's alright; and who knows, maybe happy as well"

When Joe sat down for tea on Friday night he realised that Maude was missing so asked, "Where the hell's our Maude? Don't tell me she's run off an' all. Where the hell is she?"

"No silly, she gone to stay with Dora for the

weekend. Dora's Dad got a couple of free tickets to a film or show or something in Leeds. It wasn't the sort of show that he and his wife were keen to see so he gave them to Dora. She'll be back home on Monday night. I made her catch up with the laundry and ironing before she went. She'll be ok and anyway she needed a break from all the worry about our Billy. Now he's gone she has realised how good he was to her; and us for that matter." With tears starting to roll down her face Ethel pushed away the rest of her meal, got up from the table and went to sit in her favourite armchair where she burst into uncontrollable sobs. She had kept all this bottled up until now but there was no stopping it. She sobbed and howled her heart out until Joe eventually took her in his arms and tried to console her anguish. Saying, "You sit there lass, I'll brew up a nice cup of tea, that will make you feel better. Tomorrow we'll go out and look for him again. He can't be very far away. He wouldn't want to ride too far in his condition, especially pulling his trailer."

"I don't know about that Joe. He was very upset and he's scared to death in case you belt him again, you must have really hurt him, both physically and mentally, especially that last time when he had done nothing wrong at all. He was always going off for long walks in the fields and woods and no one said he couldn't. You didn't say he had to go the youth club again for Maude's sake. She has always treated him like shit and he always got the blame. Well it dammed well served her right. It's a pity that our Billy got the blame for it though. He didn't deserve any of the blame and now we're suffering for it. I've just realised it will be his birthday in a week or two I hope to god he will be here for that day. I've already bought him a gear set for his meccano outfit and the latest famous five book, by Enid Blyton."

"Aye well, you're probably right about all that love, but we can't do owt about it now can we? When we get him back things will be a lot different around here I can tell you. Our Maude got life far too easy. I'd 'ave been better off putting my belt across her arse instead of Billy's. She should be helping you here in the house, not Billy, He has enough to do outside. What with the pigs and sugar beet, firewood and coal, not to mention the garden and hens."

Joe wasn't at all happy with his own behaviour either. He realised he should have taken a lot more notice of the arrangements inside his home and not left all that to Ethel. He had just assumed that Maude was just as keen a helper as Billy had been and just as willing to help out. Instead, Ethel had been left with it all as well as her full time job at the factory. No wonder she was tired out, coming home every night to all the cooking, laundry and cleaning. Meanwhile, when Maude wasn't lazing around in the house she was skiving off to her friends place for a free night out. Ethel must have given her some spending money as well. Just wait 'til that little madam comes home on Monday night, there would have to be big sorting out, that's for sure. Even when Billy was at home he should have attended to it but now it was imperative that he sorted it out for Ethel's sake. He had accepted that with Billy gone, he himself would have to move up a gear to fill the gaps outside and that lazy bitch Maude would have to assist Ethel in the house or else she would be severely dealt with.

Joe and Ethel spent most of the weekend searching everywhere but they were running out of options. They took time out to talk to service station attendants, traffic controllers or anyone else likely to observe passing traffic. It would not, surely, be possible for a bicycle outfit towing, a fair sized trailer to pass through any town or village without someone noticing it. Even if Billy was smart enough to travel only by night his bicycle outfit would stick out like a sore thumb. Someone must have noticed a bicycle towing a trailer and discussed it with their friends and relatives. The outfit was so unusual, even bizarre.

Of course, the reason for no-one sighting Billy or his bicycle was that it never existed on the roads in Yorkshire, or any of the adjoining counties, after Billy stopped collecting sugar beet. Finding and utilising a night travelling low loader was a great stroke of good fortune for Billy, and let's face it he certainly needed a stroke of good luck in his miserable life. By about teatime on Sunday they'd had enough so they went back home to drink lots of strong tea and console each other before they went to bed. During the last few weekends, all they had achieved was to alienate most of their friends and relatives, even Joe's mother and sister were hostile towards Joe. The farm hand Hubert who worked with Joe feeding the cattle on Sunday morning was giving him a cold shoulder. Every Sunday morning after the second feed the two of them had gotten into the habit of going for a long walk through the nearby fields and woods hunting for game such as rabbits and hares. Hubert was a dead eyed shot with the catapult and often shot a rabbit before Joe could get in a shot with .410 shot gun. When working in the fields he kept a wary eye on the ground to collect nice round stones for projectiles. Since Billy disappeared Hubert didn't want to have anything more to do with Joe because he was very fond of Billy and enjoyed his company on their walks.

Chapter Eleven

Billy was so busy that he had little time to spare. He was keen to go for a tour of the town and riverside. That would have to wait for a while until the café was running almost by itself. He was also keen to get out into the vegetable garden. He thought that there might be some seasonal roots and herbs to harvest. Vanessa had told him that she shared the garden with a decent old guy called Harold who managed to keep the weeds at bay but never managed much of a crop of food suitable for the café. There was a very old rundown cottage in one corner, which the old chap lived in and supplied some food crops in lieu of rent, but it was getting too much for him. He couldn't manage the heavy digging but once the ground had been worked over he was happy with the planting and weeding.

He looked after a shed full of laying hens as well and these did supply the café with all its need and even some to sell at the counter as well, and lots of fantastic manure to fertilise the garden. There was far too much manure to use for the garden alone so Harold had been heaping it up outside the sheds where it matured with natures help into a magnificent store of fertiliser.

Over the garden wall there were three small fields laid down to pasture where a neighbour ran a flock of sheep. Billy was keen to rotary hoe one field each year to grow spuds and other root vegetables that needed little care throughout the summer months. There was a Ferguson tractor in the shed and machinery to go with it that would make a root crop easy to establish and handle. That project would have to wait until next spring but he would need to spend a few days before winter set in to break up the turf and work it up to a good seed bed. One day he had a chat with the neighbour, Phillip, who leased the fields from Vanessa. He agreed that the land was desperately in need of a good tilling. It had been grazed with sheep for years so it would produce a good crop without a lot of extra fertiliser. There was plenty of hen manure that needed to be used up and Phillip offered to assist with the work for a share of the crop. He moved the sheep out of the nearest field so Billy could make a start to plough it up. He checked the tractor over, and had the battery charged ready to go. Once the battery was back in he started the tractor and attached the rotary hoe ready for work. He rotary hoed a strip around the outside of the field to remove the weeds, then prepared a single furrow plough ready to start ripping up the rest of the ground with the mouldboard plough. That much would have to do for now because he didn't want to neglect the café now that it was starting to shape up.

The current staff were good and worked well as a team but they needed a leader to keep them organised and to prevent them slipping into slovenly ways. Late one morning whilst Billy was still experimenting in the kitchen, two Indian chaps called in. Mary shuddered, she knew immediately that they were selling something and it was probably a bit shoddy and certainly something that she didn't want anything to do with. She was too busy to listen to their sales patter, however it turned out they were only looking for lunch. The Indians asked Mary about the curries and casseroles on the menu so she called Billy out to chat to them. They asked mainly about his curries. He asked them to sit down at a corner table whilst he organised samples of his latest recipes. At last he had some curry experts to test and advise him. He brought out a tray with a number of small dishes each containing samples of curry. He asked the men to taste each of them and describe the experience. Two of the dishes they said were too bland for their taste but they were nice and would suit people who were not used to hot foods such as curry. The third dish they said was much improved but still somewhat mild for their palates although good enough for them to buy a dish each for lunch. Billy smiled at that, he went back into the kitchen and brought out two steaming dishes of curry and crusty bread and butter. The men started into the curry with relish. They were hungry. After a couple of spoons full they stopped, eating, looked at one another and. broad grins appeared on both faces.

One of the men said, "What the heck is this? Where did this come from? This isn't the same as any of the samples that we tried. This is a real curry. A real Indian curry from Madras, or somewhere near there. Where did you get hold of a curry like this here in England? Is there and Indian restaurant or take away around here somewhere?"

Billy replied with a big smile on his face, "I was hoping that you might think like that. I thank you sincerely for the complement. This is as near as you'll get to an Indian Restaurant within many miles of here. If you hadn't come in I would have thrown this lot out. I'm trying to learn how to cook Indian and Chinese takeaway meals and Thai stir-fries. I have a number of books with an assortment of recipes that I am trying out. I was quite pleased with the third sample and it will probably be good enough for the people around here but I was trying to tweak it up a bit for the connoisseurs like yourselves. I thought I had over done the spices and whilst I enjoyed it, I thought other people would not.

My staff here tried it with some reticence and mixed reactions. I was ready to feed it to my neighbours pigs or our hens then I might get curried pork or curried eggs."

"We live in Cheltenham and would be happy to travel out here for curry like this. Will you serve it in the restaurant here or only take away? We would bring our whole families here if that were possible. Here in your restaurant it will be piping hot, whereas takeaway starts to spoil as soon as you dish it up. Maybe our wives would be happy to advise you on different variations as well."

"Look guys I am experimenting with takeaway menus but I would be happy to serve you all in here. We can reserve a table to your liking and your good ladies might want to bring some samples of other Indian foods to make it into a feast. If you call in on your way home I'll put the rest of this curry into takeaway boxes for you to take home for them to try."

"That sounds like a plan. Have you got a lot more of this or is this a small trial batch? You might sell it all before we get back."

"I've realised that with this style of cooking it

is not prudent to make up small batches. The spices don't blend in together that way. You have to make up a large quantity to give the spices time to imbue themselves right through the whole mixture. Also when you taste test the mixture you need to eat quite a lot of it at once to allow your taste buds to absorb and assimilate the flavours. So I made up a large quantity and if it came to a pinch I would have tamed it down with more basic ingredients. I don't think there's any chance that I'll sell all of it before you return and if it looks like we might run short I'll put a quantity aside ready for you to collect on your way home. I do intend to try free samples of it on my customers in tasting dishes as I did for you. If you decide to come for either takeaway or dine-in meals, would it be possible for you to telephone ahead with times and numbers before you come then I can make up a fresh batch ready for you?"

"We like the sound of that mate," said the same man as before, and we will be back for sure. Now, how much do we owe you for today?"

"Oh! It's on the house. I haven't even begun to work out a pricing schedule for the takeaway yet let alone the dine-in meals. It was good to get your feedback and comments, they are worth more than mere money to me, thanks. I can go ahead with some confidence now, thank you so much." Billy replied.

The Indian man took out a wallet, removed some notes and gave them to Billy, saying, "The pleasure was all ours mate, it will stay with us all day. Here take this and our special thanks. We'll call in tonight, a little after 5 o'clock."

Billy was ecstatic. He hurried home as soon as he could to relate the day's events to Vanessa. "Gosh Billy, I don't know where you get it all from. There must be a line of chefs in your heritage somewhere mate." Giving him a king sized cuddle and a kiss on the cheek. I'll make a cup of tea then we need to have a great big talk, said Vanessa. Once the tea was served they both sat down at the table, sipping the hot strong tea and eating some of Vanessa's scones.

Chapter Twelve

"Ok Billy, truth time in strict confidence. Because I am your Boss and you are living in my house I really do need to know who you are. Anything you say here will remain in confidence, just between us for now. Sergeant Robins has let things go on for a while but now but he needs to know the truth of who you actually are, where you've come from, and why. We both believe the scars on your back tell us why you're here and because they are so savage and sadistic we'll both protect you to the limit. You've proved to us that you are a hard working, smart, diligent, young man and deserve a second chance, no matter what you've done, so come on open up, please."

"Ok Boss I am scared stiff of what might become of me after you hear my story but to save a lot of mucking about in the future I think

Sergeant Robins should be in on this. Maybe his WPC, Acton, I think it was, might like to take notes as well. You're probably about to lose a good worker and a 'chef' before this day is out, but if you're prepared for that outcome, ring the police station, now so we can make a start. Vanessa had a very stern look on her face as she rang Sergeant Robins. She turned to Billy and said they're on their way."

Once the Sergeant and WPC arrived Vanessa took everyone into the dining room. Sergeant Robins studied Billy's face for a moment and the anguish that he was going through was plain to see. He opened with, "Please try and relax Billy. I can see how painful this for you and having seen your wounds I can understand your anguish. We can all band together to help you through this mess and we are going to do that. WPC Acton here will record everything we say but it will be on plain paper and will not go into the official files. So when you're ready just begin, and tell us in your own time please."

Billy began by telling the Sergeant about his home life leading up to the savage brutality that made him escape from his home. He then went through the scenario of the social club and the savage beltings that he had received as a result. He told them of his departure from home and the good fortune in finding a suitable mode of transport to get as far away from the area as possible and as quickly as possible. He told them of his concerns regarding the speed of his chosen mode of travel [only about 8 or 10 miles per hour on average] before realising that it was much faster than on his bike. Another facet of this mode of travel was the continuity of movement for more than twenty hours per day plus the fact that he didn't need to do anything to make it happen. Once he found the folded tarpaulins he fell asleep because he was exhausted having hardly slept at all since the first beltings and relieved to be away from it all, he hoped. He mentioned the roundabout near Leeds then the ones near Sheffield and Birmingham. He realised that he must leave the low loader somewhere convenient, to continue onwards. It would have to be at a fuel and meal stop.

He explained about the AA handbook which described the roadhouse here.

Coming from a farming background he felt the need to dismount here or somewhere similar where there may be shelter in old farm buildings and if he was lucky, find some farm work. He told them he was quite competent in most farming work including driving a tractor. He was hoping to dismount from the low loader when the crew stopped for a meal which he realised they were overdue for. The danger part was in unloading his bike and trailer without being seen. As it was he was almost caught out. He thought he might have to abandon his rig and escape on foot if he was seen as he nearly was. He said he thought that the steady pouring rain had been a help to cover his exit from the lorry. He then told them he had just had his birthday prior to the new school year starting so he did not have to worry about that although as soon as he was more settled he intended to find a place in the technical college in Cheltenham or somewhere close enough to ride his bike. He was hoping to get some formal qualifications in book keeping and business management as well as gourmet cooking. He was already well versed in mathematics but a little more might help.

It was a very long involved story and he finally stopped for another cup of tea and more scones. The police shook hands with him and Vanessa then left. Billy dived into his gourmet cook book and switched his mind into another world. Later that night after they'd had a shower and were enjoying a final cup of cocoa, Vanessa realised they had been duped. She said, "That was an amazing journey Billy thank goodness you got clean away and were lucky enough to find my café at a desperate time when I would have done anything to get some help. I will always be thankful for that."

"You have to realise Boss, that the deal went both ways. I needed you just as much, maybe a good deal more than you needed me." Vanessa stood up to clear away the pots when she suddenly turned to Billy and gave him a cuddle and another kiss on his cheek before he said, "Good night Boss see you in the morning."

As he was stepping through the doorway into the passage Vanessa called out, "Hey! You cunning little monkey. You told us all that poly-waffle of a story as a smoke screen, we still have no idea where you came from or who you are or how old you are." Billy turned around to face Vanessa with the cheekiest grin imaginable across his sweet little face, "If it helps Boss, I'm one year older than I was when I arrived here. "Goodnight Vanessa." Vanessa couldn't help herself. Once Billy was out of sight she turned away and sat down for a good old laugh whilst thinking to herself, "The cheeky little monkey. He might only be a kid but he's about three steps ahead of us lot." She rinsed out their mugs before heading off upstairs to her Bed.

When Vanessa woke the next morning she couldn't help herself and let her hair down for another good giggle, just as Billy came up with a mug of tea for her. "Tell me the joke Boss so I can have a giggle with you." he said.

"Not on your life." she remarked. "It was only a girlie joke, not suitable for a young man like you. Go get some breakfast on the go."

"Already done that, Boss. Sausages, bacon, 2 eggs, fried bubble and squeak and fried bread. If you don't hurry up you'll have to eat it in the nick before it gets cold." Billy left her to her ablutions as he prepared to serve their meal. They had gotten into the habit of eating two large meals per day because there is nothing more frustrating than trying to eat beautifully cooked food whilst doing business in the café, so they only picked and sampled during the day.

"During breakfast Vanessa asked, "What have you got in line for today, mate?"

"I'm going to rotary hoe the spud patch to break up all the lumps left by the plough. Phillip has been helping old Harold to cart and spread most of that old hen manure and it needs digging in. They left some of the very oldest manure and stacked it neatly against a wall to start seedlings off. Phillip had quite a pile of mixed manure at his place and a friend of his runs a fairly big piggery and he is always in trouble trying to find homes for all the pig manure so I restored the old farm cart and changed it so that we can tow it behind the Ferguson tractor. Phillip is the only one who has a license to drive it. By the time that the frosts have cleared we should be ready to plant all those seed spuds I got from Scotland. I've been looking through the machinery catalogues for a two row planter to go on the linkage of the tractor. We might have to import a Dutch machine that is easily converted to plant greens like cauliflowers and cabbages. It has grippers that hold the plants, lowers them into the ground, and back fills the rows, all in one go." If we plant the seeds in the greenhouse once it is repaired they will be ready to plant out before we plant the spuds

"Hey Boss, you know how one end of the first field has a high stone and brick wall along the road and down the house side, do you have any idea what that was used for. It might have been a large barn or cart shed maybe?"

"No mate, I can't help you there. It has always been like that in my day. Why are you concerned about an old wall? Is it likely to collapse or something?"

"Heck, no Boss. It's as sound as a rock. The reason I asked is that the ground that it surrounds is all stone and mortar and next to useless. I just thought that it would make a good back wall for another greenhouse, a really big one. I was talking to Phillip the other day and he knows of a very big, but neglected greenhouse fairly close by. He wondered if we could remove most, or all of the glass panes and remove it. The elderly farmer who owns it has to get rid of it to build houses but no-one seems interested. He's tried to sell it but could find no takers. We reckon that we can separate the two halves and make them into lean-to greenhouses against those walls. The soil there is useless for normal agriculture. Apart from all the rocks the earth beneath them has been dead for many years. It might come good eventually given enough time whereas we can build a greenhouse on it because we change the soil annually. Reclaiming the glass will take time then we would need plenty of putty to refit the panes. I believe we can remove the glass quite quickly as the old putty is cracked and dead. Once they are deglazed they will dismantle and transport easily. It'll need very little cash just labour. If we hire a fork lift and a lot of palettes the panes can be placed straight onto palettes for transport. Phillip reckons he can spare plenty of time at the moment and his team are keen to help. The owner needs a decision quickly so the developers can make a start, and don't forget it won't cost us a single penny piece only removal costs.

"Talking about our old green house, Billy. How bad is it? How much do you think it will cost to repair? How long will it be before that repair can be done?"

"The woodwork is ok, needs a bit of paint though, main problem is the glass. It looks as though some kids have been using it for target practice. Most of the broken panes are on the end around the doorway. That means they'll be easy to repair. I have asked the plumber and the carpenter for a quote but it's only a minor repair and I can do it myself if they are too greedy. Being as it is on the vertical wall it will be simple. They can supply the glass cut to size then all I need is a container of putty. I will only need two of the end walls off the other greenhouse, three at the most so there will be some glass from there if it happens to be the same size As soon as it's repaired I'll arrange to get 100 tomato plants, put in the hangers to support them and some new soil mix.

During the following week Billy went over to chat with Phillip. He told Phillip that he had been thinking about the soil for the greenhouse because it would need fresh dirt free of fungus and weeds if possible. They went for a stroll along the river-bank where they found a decent supply of washed coarse sand. They reckoned that about one third of that mixed with a similar amount of good quality loamy topsoil and lots of leaf mould and manure. There was a heavy layer of leaf mould in among the trees in the nearby woods that could easily be raked up and there was a good supply of the oldest hen manure beneath the big heap outside the shed. In one of the buildings there was a great big concrete mixer which, provided the motor still ran ok they could use to mix the ingredients. Phillip was a little concerned that there wouldn't be enough fertiliser in the mix to mature a growth of tomatoes. There was a tap inside the end of the green house and Billy said they would set up a 44gal drum beneath it to supply the plants with water. It was important that the tomatoes were watered with warm water not cold water run out of a hose pipe to obtain maximum growth. That meant they could half fill a spud bag with mixed manure and lower it into the drum on a piece of rope after each watering, turn the tap on and refill the drum ready for the next watering. The bag would be lifted out to drain then a watering can could be used to ladle out the water to feed the tomato plants.

Phillip said, "It sounds to me as though you've done this before Billy."

"Yes, and it worked well, although it means hand watering twice each day. On the farm in Yorkshire where I grew up we did it every year like that. We put in new top soil every year to eliminate fungus and diseases. I'm quite sure that we never lost a single tomato plant. We removed all the side shoots and restricted the plants to only 5 main trusses of fruit."

"If you can make time, and I can, let's set a date to measure and remove enough glass from the new house then repair the old one. Time is short so get your crew together mix up some soil whilst you and I sort out the painting and glass."

"Will tomorrow be soon enough for you William. Come on let's measure the glass now then one of us can go and get some paint and putty. They found out that the glass panes in both greenhouses were identical in width and length. The old glass was a little thinner than the new one and would therefore need to be handled with a good deal more care. All the framework seemed to be sound needing only repriming and painting. Billy and Phillip travelled to the new greenhouse in Phillip's Morris shooting brake and began to remove some of the old putty off the panes in the end walls, remove the glass and carefully pack it into the shooting break. Glass especially this thicker type was very heavy so the Morris soon had as much as it could carry safely. The glass was taken to the old garden and placed carefully ready for the paintwork to be completed. Load by load they removed and relocated all the glass from the end walls then started on the vertical sidewalls. The hardest part was to remove and lower the roof panes until the farmer offered his ancient fork lift which was a great help. They found a narrow strip of heavy plywood to lay on a palette to stand on then they could work through the middle on that and lay the panes as they came of on either side of their feet. Once each palette was heavy enough it was placed on the tray of the trailer and replaced with another empty pallet and the plywood. They were going to need quite a lot more palettes until they could start refitting the panes of glass once the paint was dry. The builder who had erected the brick wall was on hand to assist with dismantling the wooden framework, transporting it and re-erecting it.

Once they got the ball rolling it quickly gained momentum. Having the fork lift quickly elevated the operation and prevented any breakages. Every spare moment they could scrounge both of their own time and the outside workers who willingly offered to work plenty of overtime to speed the job along. Once the trailer was loaded they drove the forklift to the new site to unload the pallets of glass. Some of Phillip's gang pitched in to help the painter who was slowing down the operation somewhat. Removing the rest of the old putty and any loose paint was a bigger job than any of them realised but the team was soon beginning to refit the panes of glass as soon as the paint was dry enough to take the putty. They were all very pleased with the way it was going and William ordered punnets of well established seedling tomato plants from a highly recommended grower. Even though the season was marching on a bit it was still not too late and these plants would come to fruition after the others in the old greenhouse which should spread the harvest well into early autumn.

William was somewhat concerned with Vanessa's bank balance due to the massively expensive few weeks even though they were managing to achieve a great deal on a shoestring budget. The casual wages bill was high but what the heck, not a single penny had been wasted. It was almost tax time and Vanessa needed to balance the books, pay all the bills and her income tax bill. One afternoon William went home to the farm earlier than usual, hoping to catch up with Vanessa for a serious chat about finances. When he arrived home Vanessa was sitting at the dining room table surrounded by books and papers. Her accountant was sitting opposite looking quite pleased with himself. William immediately brought up the subject of bank balances and financial affairs. Vanessa's accountant James, took another sip of his tea before telling William that the new annex and hot houses along with the machinery from Holland had saved the day. Investment allowances had balanced the books very nicely and the income tax saved would go a long way towards the new work and machinery.

Chapter Thirteen

By the time Billy had organised to plant a vegetable crop with Phillip and Harold's help a few more weekends had passed by without Joe or Ethel seeing or hearing about Billy's demise or his whereabouts. They hadn't had any inklings of his possible hideout. Surely by now someone must have seen him or his bike rig. He had to live and eat somewhere. Where was he getting the support he needed for that. Even if he was scavenging for food or worse still stealing food or money to buy food he must have been seen. Much belatedly, Joe finally went to the local police station in Barrestown because Billy had so many friends in the town it was the most likely place to hide. Joe had to endure a very unpleasant interview with the police who gave him a hard time. Although he gave them a severely edited version of his dealings with Billy it was obvious to the police that they were only getting a small part of the story. However they took down all the information, made out a report to be circulated around the county then warned Joe; that if and when Billy was found he would be under police protection and a thorough investigation would ensue with the possibility of criminal charges being laid against him. Joe had not accepted, of course, that he had actually committed a crime that would and could be punishable by law. After all, let's not forget that Billy is Joe's son and as such Joe had the right to punish him in any way he felt fit, without giving him any chance to defend himself. Because of his belief that he was right and Billy was wrong Joe spat out at the police sergeant, "What the hell are you talking about? Billy is still my son and I have the right to belt his arse whenever I feel like it so don't you threaten me." The police sergeant's hackles rose up on the back of his neck. He was ready to do battle.

Pulling himself up to his full height the sergeant addressed Joe, saying, "Joseph

Charles O'Leary, I hereby warn you that anymore talk like that or any attempt to belittle or harm your son William, or Billy as he is better known, you will be arrested and charged with threatening behaviour and contempt of court. Your son William O'Leary is formally in police custody as from now and therefore under protection of the court system. I advise you to leave this station immediately, go home and reflect on your attitude and behaviour before you end up in serious trouble, even prison."

Joe decided that discretion was the better part of valour, turned away from the counter and stepped outside. He couldn't win this battle so he headed off home to lick his wounds and report back to Ethel. It was Ethel who was copping the brunt of all this aggravation. When Joe arrived back home he was still furious. He said to Ethel, "Bugger that bloody kid. I will kill the little sod once I find him. Who the hell does he think he is, causing me all this trouble? You know lass, that bloody police sergeant gave me hell. He threatened to have me arrested and thrown in gaol if I so much as said a word against our Billy, let alone hurt him or punished him in anyway. He reckons that Billy is now under police protection whether they find him or not. I can't believe that a son of mine could do that to me. Even if we, or they find Billy he will not be allowed to live with us. They'll foster him out to someone who'll give him a nice, home away from us. All these years of hard work have been for nowt. Just when I need him he pulls a stunt like this."

Ethel was in the habit of going shopping at the open-air markets in Barrestown held every week. One week about a month after Joe's humiliation by the police she called at the police station and asked the desk sergeant what had happened about Billy's case. Had they had any news of him? Did they know if he was safe or where he might be?

The sergeant told her that they had canvassed every police station, firstly throughout the West Riding of Yorkshire without any results so the search had been widened to cover all the police stations in the whole of Yorkshire and now they were waiting for any possible results of that extended search but they did not expect to have any good news for her at the moment.

They were fairly sure that neither Billy nor his unusual bike rig had been seen anywhere in Yorkshire. However the information about Billy and his bike and trailer was now being circulated around the whole country. Thankfully Billy had made the decision to dismantle the trailer rig away from his bike. He had stored the trailer and the towbar arrangement away in one of the horseboxes on Vanessa's farm where it was not likely to be found. Of course neither Billy nor his machine could have been seen in Yorkshire because of his mode of escape. He was well outside Yorkshire, or any of the adjoining counties by the time he climbed out of the low loader. There had only ever been one sighting of them, that was outside Haversby roadhouse, and in pouring rain and very poor visibility one very dark night.

There was no wonder that Joe and Ethel couldn't find any trace of Billy. They were looking in the wrong places. Billy's bike, of course, had completely disappeared from sight into an old farm shed some 200 miles outside their search zone. Even Billy himself was melting into the back ground due to a sudden and severe change of clothing and even his demeanour. His new threads, bow tie and a special hairstyle had all added up to a change in personality. No longer was he a useless down trodden school kid with only half a brain. He was a solid, upstanding, teenage 'chef', and he walked around proud of the fact that at last he had been allowed to mature. He found it hard to believe that everyone around him now respected him and his ability in the kitchen and in the business. He no longer got insults and abuse thrown at him almost daily and by the one person who should have loved and revered him. No one ever took the piss out of him or belittled him. Best of all, he no longer got shit belted out of him on a regular basis. He seemed to have grown taller in stature and he was surely stacking on quite a few pounds of flesh around his skinny frame. Life was really good for William these days.

Chapter fourteen

One of Vanessa's problems was, how to pay Billy and how much. She decided to award him not only for his hard physical work hours but also extra rewards for his brilliance and diligence in re-establishing the café, replanning the menu and bringing everything up to date. She was only too aware that the profits were now pouring in and she wanted to share that with him. Apart from his food and accommodation she had completely refurbished his wardrobe. He now owned a number of very smart upmarket outfits as well as his uniforms. However Billy was accumulating a large cache of money that was becoming a concern. She encouraged him to visit a local bank and deposit most of it safely away. The local bank manager was a good friend of Vanessa and she was now putting much larger sums of money through in his name as well as her own.

Reluctantly, Billy went to the bank and asked for the manager. First he needed a full name and address before he could get past the front counter and gain admittance through to the manager's office. Billy was very reluctant to do this of course. The teller wasn't at all helpful, she needed full Christian names and surname as well as his address before she could take him through to the manager's office and introduce him to the manager. Eventually he had little option, he walked out of the bank, hopped on his bike and returned to the farm. Vanessa was surprised at his early return, asking him, "How did your interview at the bank go, mate? Have you got a bank account number there now?"

He told her, "No. Like I told you it's impossible unless I own up to who I am and where I come from. I didn't even get passed the snotty bitch at the front counter. I'll just have to keep on stuffing it into my mattress or somewhere."

Vanessa replied, "Oh come on mate, you can't do that. We can sort this out. Leave it to me. I'll talk to the manager, he's a nice man. There must be some way of doing this, trust me. Come on pal there's no need to upset yourself."

Billy was upset, very upset. He went out into the garden and bumped into old Harold, who could see how upset he was. He said, "Come for a walk mate. Tell me about what you're going to be planting in the field come springtime. This will be a very exciting year for us all, pal."

"Not for me it won't," Billy replied. "I won't be around to see it. I'm going to have to leave here soon."

"What the heck are you talking about mate? What's happened to upset you like this? Have you and Vanessa had some sort of a row."

"No, of course not, we're great pals. It's all about my past. It's catching up with me fast then I'll be dragged away from here. My old man will kill me if he gets hold of me. I don't want to go back there ever. At least this time I have a decent outfit to wear and some cash to help me get settled somewhere else, but I will have to move on."

As a result of her chat with Billy, Vanessa invited the bank manager over to the farm for morning tea a few days later. Billy was very apprehensive about the interview but realised the inevitability of it. Once tea and Vanessa's fabulous scones had been served along with large dish of strawberry jam and another of freshly whipped cream she carefully explained the situation regarding Billy's past. Jeffrey, the bank manager, suggested a suitable arrangement. He asked straight out, "Right Billy, short for William of course? "Yes?" Billy nodded and admitted that was correct. "How old are you Billy? I must have your exact age and birthday. I must point out that your file, account details, balances etc, will always remain strictly confidential. The police can obtain that information but only with an official search warrant and with great reluctance on the bank's behalf. Vanessa has told me that you have recently had a birthday event. Did that make you 15 years old or not?"

"No, not quite, Sir, actually I was only 14 at that time. I needed to leave school to enable me to get a full time job. As it has turned out I could have worked my shifts at the roadhouse and attend full time school although it would have been a real struggle. If I was already 15 years old I would have no problems living here. As a 15 year old I become free to leave my parents home and live anywhere within reason. Because I have a secure income and this lovely house to live in, I can't see how my dad can still drag me back to his home into what amounts to slavery and brutality."

"In view of the brutality that you suffered at the hands of your father there is no way that the courts would force you to do that, however it might help if Vanessa is prepared to adopt you and you change your name to Riley. How would you feel about that?"

"I'am loving living here with Vanessa. I have never been this well off in my whole life. The work here is hard and constant and challenging but she pays me well. My home here is very much better than I have ever imagined it could be. Vanessa and I always get on so well together. We have never had any arguments. The only issue between us is my past so if we can resolve that, and Vanessa is prepared to vouch for me, there will be no more problems between us."

"You don't need to worry about my part in

all this mate. I need you and I am prepared to pay you well as soon as we can get you a bank account." Said Vanessa with a huge grin on her face. "I never managed to have any kids of my own as you both know and I actually get to see what I am getting. Even though you are a cheeky little monkey. I'd love to adopt you Billy, mate"

"Do you know what a 'Justice of the Peace' or JP as they are generally known as, attends to Billy? For your next step you will need one at least."

"Not really, Sir, except that it is to do with legal matters." Said Billy.

"The good news on that front young man is that I am one and Michael the butcher' who you know, is too. Unfortunately we are supposed to have known you for a certain length of time but in view of the situation and the fact that two of us are prepared to acknowledge and vouch for you we can make it happen."

"What you're saying Sir, is, I assume, that you are quite happy with this but how can you vouch for Michael?"

"Aha you don't miss much young man. I

suspected that something like this was coming up so Michael and I got together and checked your background. I asked Vanessa how much she had been told and she was very vague with only limited knowledge of your history. She broke a confidence which was a bit naughty of her but only because she was talking to JP's who she knew she could trust and looking out for your welfare. We assured her it would go no further. You left a couple of name tapes on your shirts which she washed and you left your school satchel open. Written inside the flap is a grammar school and a farm address. We made very discreet enquiries around both of those addresses, pleading for information about a missing persons post by the Yorkshire police. We were able to check to see if you had ever been reported to police around those addresses. As you well know you have no history with the police and the headmaster at the Grammar School you attended gave us a glowing report of your general behaviour and your scholastic records. He also said that he was very upset about your disappearance and he would be delighted to have you back. We made sure not to leave a suspicious trail and as long as you behave here and do not get into any trouble you are safe. Now because of your age I am going to suggest a trust account with my bank with Vanessa and Michael as trustees. You will be able to draw small amounts out of it by yourself but any major withdrawals will need to have both of their signatures. So do you agree, Billy?"

"It sounds as though I no longer have any secrets and I was so careful, before I was discovered by my illustrious Boss here. As a result there is no reason not to accept and thank you and Michael, Mr Jeffrey. I might have to have strong words with my Boss though. Giving away such confidences, how naughty can she get, even though it was in my best interests with a fantastic outcome. I suppose that I need to revisit your bank again to sign some papers and register my signature for your records, is that right."

"Yes that's correct Billy and I'll set in motion your adoption papers and change of name application. Don't forget young man that from today your name is William Riley."

"Yes of course, and thank you again and good day to you Sir." Replied William.

After Mr. Jeffrey left William turned to Vanessa and looked her straight in the eyes saying, "Well young lady, what do you have to say for yourself?"

The lady in question burst into tears and held out her hands to be loved. William obliged willingly saying that he unconditionally forgave her for her sins and respected her right to do what she had done to protect herself as well as him.

The following week William telephoned the bank to make an appointment to see Mr. Jeffrey. The appointed time was 2pm so William turned up on the dot. This time there was no hold up at the counter and a very polite young lady ushered him through to the manager's office. Mr. Jeffrey stood up to greet him and invited him to sit down in front of the desk. He smiled at William before saying, "I have some good news for you today William. Your new account is ready to go. We only need a specimen signature to set it up. Have you thought about how you would like to sign for your transactions."

"Yes" William said showing Mr. Jeffrey the paper sample that he had brought with him. "I hope this will make it work."

"The signature that you wish to use is up to you and this will work well for us. Now I just need you to sign where I have marked the form. Do you wish to deposit any money into your account today?"

"Yes please, I had a fair amount stashed away and Vanessa has just paid my wages for last week as well."

"Ok William, you can deposit that with the tellers as you leave the bank."

"Well done Billy that gets you off to a good start, congratulations. He stood up and reached across the desk and shook William's hand.

"Now, William Riley, I have here a deed confirming your new name as 'William Riley' which we both need to sign."

"What happened about the adoption? Is that likely to be ok? Do I now lose my old name and become William or maybe Willy?" Billy asked.

"Yes Michael and myself have worked on the application forms and submitted them to the court. There may be some delay because they have to make a number of checks to make sure, but they are quite happy to allow it to protect you from more violence. You will be issued with a new birth certificate but how you want people to address you in the future is up to you, however to protect your anonymity I would advise you to drop the name Billy and maybe try William for now. That makes it all very simple. That was a clever move that you made to remember to collect your birth certificate before you left home. I'll let Vanessa know when the forms come back then we'll meet again for more signatures. Well, that completes today's business so I will say good afternoon to you William until we meet again soon. Thank you once again for your banking business." They shook hands again and an ecstatic 'William' walked out of the office. He noticed this time the deferential reception from the tellers as he paid in his savings and left the bank. He felt like sticking his finger up his nose then realised that that was the sort of gesture that Billy might use, where as William was much too sophisticated to indulge in such trivialities. After all, let's not forget, he had to interact with these people from now on and this was an excellent start for the future. William was a man of stature now, with a bank account and a new name.

What he needed now was an upmarket bicycle to go with his new image. He decided to ride into Cheltenham to check out the bike and sport stores to see what was available. It would be more than two years before he could obtain a licence to drive a car although he had learnt years ago, and could easily have passed a test now, which meant that he needed a good bike to fill in the gap. He rode into Cheltenham and spent all morning looking around the shops until he had a windfall. A seventeen year old young man was just leaving one of the shops as William was about to enter. He was very upset about something so William asked, "What's upset you on a lovely sunny day like this? You look as mad as hell."

"Not surprising really. Dealing with these bandits would make a parson mad. Look pal, I bought this bike of mine in this shop last year. I paid him a lot of money for it. Well yesterday I got my driver's licence and need a bit more cash for a deposit on a Morris Minor car. I expected a good price for it. It's like new as you can see. That thieving bastard only offered me less than half of what it's worth. I know it has devalued since I bought it but not that much. He has a similar bike in the showroom there that is priced at nearly what I paid him for this one. What do you reckon pal is it as good as that one in there?

William asked, "Is there a coffee bar near here where we can have a chat? I might be able to help a bit because I am looking for a good bike to replace this old banger of mine. It's been a good bike but it has nearly had the bomb."

The two young men found a nice café where they bought drinks and cakes and sat down for a chat. The end result was William agreed to buy the bike and explained the money situation. He got the bike for the difference between the asking price and the dealer's price making it a good deal for both of them. William arranged to collect and pay for the bike two days later giving him plenty of time to arrange the money with his trustees. The new bike was at the top of the range with ten speed derailer gears. The tyres were as good as new and the dynamo lights worked well. Even a brand new bike would not have been any better and with all the extras a good deal more expensive. It had pannier bags fitted over the rear wheel and drop down racing handlebars. William was thrilled. The bike was a steal and no mistake. He arranged to take a bus ride into town in a day or two to pay for and pick up the bike. First of course he had to visit Michael at the butcher's shop because he would need his signature to collect the money. Michael was quite happy to sign the papers, as was Vanessa. William still had lots left in his new bank account. He parked the old bike in the horsebox with his trailer before hopping on the bus to collect the new bike.

Chapter Fifteen

Around this time the O'Leary family, [what was left of it] up stakes and moved away from the farm after many years. Joe had a new job and a house in a nearby village. The house was a very old farm house that had never been renovated or updated. There was no bathroom or water closet. It had an old thunder box in an out building which was the case with most of the older houses in the village. One of the main reasons for the move was for Ethel and Maude's convenience. Ethel was working full time in a factory in the next village. Maude had finished school and needed to find employment. Living at the farm, daily commuting was impossible. The only bus service catered only for high school children of the district. The O'Leary family soon settled into their new abode such as it was and Maude found employment in the offices of a motor dealership in a nearby town. Ethel and Maude were pleased to have a bus stop outside the front door and a regular bus service. Bath time was a problem for Maude. A tin bath in front of the fire was not ideal for a teenage girl but Joe and Ethel never ever took a bath in the previous house anyway even though it did have a bathroom and unlimited hot water, so long as Billy chopped the fire wood.

One day the postman knocked on the door. When Ethel opened the door to him he proffered an official looking envelope with the comment, "You are Mrs, Ethel O'Leary are you, love? I have a registered letter for you and you, or Joseph O'Leary have to sign for it". He offered the receipt document and Ethel signed it. She was completely mystified as to what the connection between her, her husband Joe, and the county court in Worcester might be. She took the letter indoors and sat down at the table to open the letter. Then it suddenly dawned on her, this must be something to do with their Billy. Somebody might have found him. Oh God, don't tell me that something has happened to him? Has he been arrested or is he in hospital? There were a lot of pages of official writing before she got to the nitty gritty of the letter. She had guessed straight away that it would have something to do with their Billy and she was correct. It appeared that Billy had applied to the court for permission to change his surname to Riley and a Mrs. Vanessa Riley [who ever she was] had applied to the court for permission to adopt William and provide him with a suitable home. The court had approved all this in due consideration of the sadistic brutality that he'd been subjected to apparently at the hands of one "Joseph Charles O'Leary. Having satisfied themselves that the applicants were of sound mind and disposition the court had agreed to honour their plea. Furthermore, after extensive checks had been carried out, the court thoroughly endorsed the actions. Mrs. Vanessa Riley was in fact a successful business entrepreneur and the owner and proprietor of a thriving business. These court orders will come fully into law after 90 days during which time the O'Leary family could lodge a counter claim. However, should such a claim ensue, Joseph Charles

O'Leary would be immediately arrested and charged with multiple cases of assault and battery against one William O'Leary, his son. Ethel broke down and burst into tears calling out loudly, "Oh! Joe what have you done to us? Our Billy didn't deserve any of the beltings that you gave him and now we've lost him forever. She wondered how the heck Billy managed to get all that way on his bike. She thought that it must be every bit of two hundred miles away. She realised that she would have to show the letter to Joe when he came in and he would go berserk with Ethel copping the brunt of blame as usual. She had dearly loved Joe and they had been through some very hard times together but this was all too much to bear. She felt that she should leave him but she had nowhere to go. She realised just how their Billy must have felt, cornered and trapped. How could she get away and where could she go? If she left, Joe would not let her stay. He would seek her out and destroy her, mentally if not physically. Then she had Maude to consider. What would happen to her if she left? Poor Ethel she was totally bereft. Completely shattered and she had no friends in the village to help her out. No one to even discuss it with, not even when their Maude came home after work, because she would be worse than useless.

Ethel just placed the letter on the dining table next to Joe's dinner plate without making any comment. When Joe sat down to eat he picked up the letter, and said. "What the bloody hell is this about Ethel. Is it summat to do with our Billy. It looks very official. It's from the county court of Worcester."

Ethel answered him, "Yes it's about Billy, but he's not our Billy anymore so you'd better read what it says."

She then burst into tears and began to cry her eyes out. She was inconsolable. Joe jumped up saying "Now then lass don't take on so. There's nowt in there that we can't put right. There's no need to upset yourself like this, love."

Through her tears and sobs Ethel said, "You'd better have a look at the letter before you say anymore. We've lost our Billy and we can't do anything about it because they will arrest you and put you in prison if you try. Please Joe read that letter before you say any more."

Joe picked up the letter and pulled out the contents. As he settled down to read through it all he got madder and madder. He was ready to explode and explode he did. "What the bloody hell are they playing at, them buggers have known all along where our Billy was hiding. I feel like going to Barrestown and giving that bloody copper a piece of my mind, but what's the bloody use. They didn't even listen to me before. He threatened to have me arrested before when I went in there and now it's official. Bugger it all Ethel they can have the little sod. I'm wiping my hands of the whole affair. He can rot in hell as far as I'm concerned. He'd better not get himself into any trouble 'cause he won't get any help around here I can tell you that. We could spend a lot of time looking for him then get arrested for our troubles, so that's 'tend of it and good riddance I say.

The next morning Joe got his own breakfast He was heading off for a day's threshing. The farmer's wife supplied all their meals. He was going to Tollerton which was a long drive away. He needed an early start to get the machine set up for 7.30 am. Ethel got out of bed around midmorning. She was still fully dressed from the day before. She fed the pigs and hens then went for a walk. She was so miserable that she didn't care where she went. Her tears were flowing freely as she left the farmyard.

Out behind the homestead the dirt road led down to a big screening plant. The whole area was a massive quarry, which produced tons of washed gravel for building and road works. The part nearest to the house had already been quarried and it was a huge lake now. The water was very deep, about 25 feet deep and the road ran very close to the water's edge. Ethel had never been able to swim in fact she did not even like walking near the lake. Once in her earlier days she was boating on a nearby river and nearly drowned when she fell overboard. Her friends were able to haul her out but she tried to avoid deep water these days. She had only lived here a few weeks and had never been out here before. She was amazed by the size of the lake, which was many acres of water. Today she was so miserable, she didn't care what happened to her. She watched the water birds paddling across the surface, then without warning she suddenly fell into the lake. The road was used by the quarry trucks only. She was all alone out there so no one saw what happened to her. No one saw her fall into the water.

When Maude returned home from work she called out for her Mum. Everything was odd. The fire was cold. Her dad generally lit it first thing but without constant fuelling it had soon gone out. Maude searched for her mother then approached the neighbours who lived across the street and the publican of the "Red Lion Pub" next door, to no avail. When Joe got home the place was in pandemonium. Half the village people were out looking, even the village copper. Joe approached him and said, "Look here you this is all your fault. You and your blasted pals started this lot, so get out there looking for our Ethel. The policeman was stunned. Of course he knew nothing of the letter from the court. He said, "I've no idea what you are talking about Joe but I'm ready to help out. It's nearly dark now so we will have to start early in the morning. Don't worry, she'll turn up, she can't have gotten far."

Just after dark a local man turned up as soon

as he heard what was going on. He drove one of the lorries from the quarry, delivering sand and gravel. Jimmy told the copper that, when he was leaving the quarry with his second load of the day, he saw someone who he assumed was Joe's wife, Ethel walking out of the farmyard in the direction of the quarry road, but thought nothing of it. It appeared that there was a fair chance that she had either fallen or tripped into the lake or was walking around out there in the quarry. The next morning most of the villagers turned out in force but there were no trace of Ethel. Eventually the search was called off with everyone thinking that she had fallen or slipped into the water. Joe confirmed that Ethel had never learnt to swim. During the next few days Timmy and all the other drivers kept a lookout along the water's edge until on the third or fourth day Timmy spotted something coloured near the edge of the water. He stopped his lorry and got down for a look. There, lying in the edge of the lake was a female body. Timmy had never met Ethel but he was sure it would turn out to be her. He climbed back into his lorry and drove it down to the council estate where the constable lived with his family. Timmy turned his lorry round and drove the policeman back to the quarry. The village policeman only had a police issue bicycle for transport. They were going to have some difficulty lifting Ethel's body out of the water and up the bank onto the road. The bank was very steep and went straight down into deep water. Neither of the men were competent swimmers so ultimate care was needed. Once the body was clear of the water they left it on the sloping bank to allow some of the water to drain from her clothing before dragging it up onto the roadway. By then more lorry drivers had arrived to help and the local message bank had started to circumnavigate the village. There was plenty of help to get Ethel's body onto one of the lorries and into Harrogate hospital for a post mortem examination.

The post mortem showed up nothing except lungs full of water. There were no physical injuries present at all. No alcohol or any other substances were present so the body was released for burial. The internment took place at Stanbeck cemetery. Joe and Maude were devastated. Maude never had any affection for her mother when she was alive but now she was so upset that she visited the cemetery every weekend for months taking bunches of flowers with her. Of course, there had to be an inquest to determine the cause of death. Accidental drowning was the only possible outcome since there was no one anywhere near Ethel when she disappeared.

Joe was going to miss his dead wife because he had always insisted on Ethel waiting on him, hand and foot, but he settled down to a life with only Maude for company and she was never as obliging as her Mum had been. He was forced into much more domestic duties and he had the live-stock to attend to. Maude was worse than useless especially outside the home, but she did pitch in and collect the daily egg harvest, clean, sort, and pack them ready for the egg board on Mondays.

After a few weeks Joe reverted to jumping over the garden wall and into the Pub next door. He didn't drink much beer but he loved to play a domino game called fives and threes and he was very good at that. He managed to win most of the beer that he drank.

As time went on Joe began to drink more and more beer and it was becoming a problem. He was seriously argumentative at best and he had a vicious temper and was apt to seriously argue a point just for the sake of it. Maude quickly got sick and tired of being the dogsbody. She was working full time yet expected to run the house as good if not better than her mum had done, and look after the poultry, collect and process the eggs for sale. Maude had no free time at all. Now she began to realise why their Billy escaped. Even without the beltings this was no life for a teenager. At least her dad had never struck her let alone took his belt to her but she knew the threat was always there. She vowed to herself that if he ever struck her she would leave although she had no idea where she might go. One lunch time when Maude was at work one of her colleagues came to chat with her. Penny unfolded her lunch and as she began to eat she asked Maude, 'Have you ever felt like moving on Maude?"

"What's sort of question is that? Moving on, to where, exactly? You mean change jobs? Leave here, then what?" She replied.

"Yes, that's exactly what I am saying. You're only paid a pittance from this mob and you're at everyone's beck and call. You could do a lot better than this."

"I suppose this silly talk is leading up to something is it." Maude retorted.

"Well yes, I have kept this a secret but there are some top jobs going over at that new factory out on the Skipton road. I've just been accepted over there and the salary is way better than here with quite a few extra perks as well."

"What are you suggesting that I take a dirty old factory job and away out there. How will I get from the bus station and back?"

"No silly, they are setting up a new office structure and looking for skilled people like you to run the place. I've been given the under manager's position because I don't have the right qualifications to take on the top job but you could do it easily, You've had the experience and know the job backwards."

"That all sounds good but there's still the problem of getting back and forth from the bus station. I don't believe there is a direct bus service to that area."

"Yes I know that and I'll have that problem too. Our place is even harder to get to and a fair bit further. Just have a look at this advert, Maude, I can't manage it on my own but if we both move in we could do it easily. It's within easy walking distance from the factory. The rent seems reasonable and the lady sounds very nice. She has recently been widowed and is lonely. There are two double bedrooms both with en-suite showers. She only uses a snug downstairs so we could have full use of the lounge room. Oh come on Maude, you are miserable living at home. Just think new job, new home, new life. What do you say?"

"It's ok for you. You have the job already. I would have to see if the job is still available and send in my resume before anything else.

"No, no, no. Here is the general manager's card. I have already done all the ground work for you. He is waiting for you to call him. The job is yours if you want it. Also I have reserved the right to the house as well. I haven't seen it but the lady is pretty desperate. If we go and see her when we knock off we can have it. Come on, what do you say? Ring that number, now."

Maude ended up doing that. The office was still empty with everyone at lunch The manager said the job was hers subject to a suitable interview. She agreed to get a taxi over there as soon as she left work and he agreed to wait for her. Penny went along with Maude to see the house if the interview went well. They arranged to share the taxi fare. When the taxi pulled up outside the factory the manager stepped out and paid the fare much to the girl's relief. The interview was very brief and mainly about travel arrangements. Imagine the manager's surprise when told about the nearby house. He stood up, shook Maude's hand and welcomed her onboard. The two girls walked around the corner and approached the front door of the massive house that was to be their new home. Alison showed them into her lovely furnished snug asking them to please be seated, which they did. They were soon made comfortable with a welcome cup of tea and a plate of homemade biscuits and cakes. The three of them settled down for a good old natter about terms and other details all of which were acceptable and readily agreed on then handshakes all round. Alison escorted them on a tour of the house. It was centrally heated from a large automatic boiler in the cellar. Alison was established in a lovely bedroom at the rear of the house overlooking the hills. It was a picture. There was a family bathroom across the hall. Back down stairs there was a beautifully fitted out laundry with a near new automatic washing machine and a drier. The lounge room was very big and well furnished and fitted out with the latest television set and stereo outfit. They only needed to bring their personal belongings and they were set up. Alison showed them the upmarket kitchen and scullery where they could make their own breakfast. She was a keen cook and wanted to organise the kitchen to cook their evening meals. Alison then rang for a taxi to take them back to the bus station. The girls had decided to move in on the Saturday. They had their own telephone in the lounge which they would be responsible for. Maude was dreading having to tell her dad that she was leaving but she had no choice. She said to Penny, "Dad will be working on Saturday. To save a massive row and maybe a good hiding, I've decided to write him a letter and leave it on the table for him when I leave. I don't intend to give him my new address and my old boss won't get it either. I've taken out a post office box number for now that should keep the wolves at bay until we get settled in. I've checked with my boss here and he's not happy but because I have a lot of holiday pay I'll finish up this Friday. I've already posted adverts for a new office manager to start immediately if possible. I will start interviews on Thursday."

"Ok Maude," said Penny, "Our Johnny is in town this weekend and will take my stuff over first thing then we'll come to Gravely and collect you and all your bits and bobs. There's bound to be far too much to lug about on the bus"

"Oh gosh you don't have to do that I can catch the bus at the front door." Replied Maude.

Penny pointed out that there would probably be more than she expects when she gets it sorted out and she had to swap buses twice. "Alright then you win. I'll be waiting for you," she said. "Don't stop out at the front gate, bring him into the yard to keep the nosey villagers out. I'll chuck in a few dozen eggs for us as well. We can live on scrambled eggs and omelettes for now. Dad will go nuts when he sees my letter but unless he is a total imbecile he must realise that I have been miserable ever since our Billy left and then Mum's death on top of all that so who cares. He hasn't made life easy for me and he treats me like shit also, so good riddance. I suppose I should be glad he never belted me."

When Joe arrived home from work he couldn't understand what had happened. The fire was cold and there was no dinner prepared ready for him. He spotted Maude's letter ripped it open and read the contents. He yelled out at the top of his voice, "Of all the ungrateful bitches, After all I did for her. She's no better than our Billy. He then stormed around the house checking her room yelling and shouting all sorts of obscenities. It finally dawned on him that, not only was he on his own but the hens and pigs had not been attended to. All the eggs were still in the nests, hens needed feeding and watering. The pigs needed to be cleaned out and fed. Joe was ropable he did not know which way to turn. After another bout of yelling and shouting he realised, that Billy was the cause of all his misery. This mess can wait. Joe climbed over the wall into the pub yard before he remembered that he was not welcome in there either and the beer was like witches piss anyway.

A few months earlier the landlord of the pub had set up the lounge bar, which had hereto had very little use It was a spacious room much larger than the public bar area and ideal to convert into a flashy dining room where they could serve gourmet meals. Their Elite customers travelled out from nearby towns and the city for a quiet night in the country. The landlady catered for the meals and put on a gourmet feast with a little help from a couple of young ladies from the village. The message soon got around and the dining room was full almost every night. They needed more tables and there were three 8 seater ones in the bar. The landlord thought he could reserve these tables for diners instead of leaving them for the local yokels who only drank a few beers and played dominoes or more especially "Five and Threes" which is an upmarket version of dominoes. When the posh city diners came in, they indulged in cocktails at the bar often ordering bottles of wine and champagne for their partners before sitting down to a three or four course meal with more wines and even spirits. The evening usually ended up with liqueurs and nightcaps as well. Joe and his friends were having none of that. They told him that it was registered as a public bar and would stay that way unless he applied to the licensing authority to change it. The landlord was determined to get rid of the local yokels so he could use it for elite dining. He explained to Joe that those tables earned five, maybe ten times as much when used for dining than when used for village yokels like him to play dominoes and drink a bit of beer. The stand-off continued until the landlord began neglecting to flush and clean the beer dispensing equipment so the beer tasted 'off' and the beer was stale. Joe and his friends lost out because they were forced to travel a couple of miles to the next village where they could get a decent pint of ale and let the elite diners take over their pub. This was the final straw for Joe. All his family had left him, his favourite pub was buggered up, and he had no one to look after him and he was all alone. He fed the livestock went back out to the barn, brought out his van and drove to the Tawnton pub nearby and settled in for a heavy night of boozing with his mates from his village. That wasn't the end of Joe's miseries. The police from town were having a bit of a blitz and they stopped him at the cross roads on the way home and charged him with drunk driving. Because of his exemplary reputation and a clear driving record the magistrate reduced the charge to 'driving under the influence of alcohol'. As a result he got off quite lightly without being arrested but he copped a heavy fine and three months suspension of his driver's licence. Bugger it that was the end he reckoned, he needed his licence to do his job. He was a tractor driver for a large agricultural contractor. He mostly drove his own van and the farm tractors, mainly on the roads. The magistrate told him that he could apply for a special licence if he could put up a good enough case to support the application he might get one. Very reluctantly, but born out of necessity, Joe sat down that night and wrote to the Magistrate. He outlined some of the family crisis and woes, promised never to transgress again. He apologised sincerely to the court and the police for his stupidity. The magistrate was suitably impressed and granted him a daylight only special licence so that he could continue working. This was a great outcome both for Joe and his boss. Joe's employment consisted in moving a threshing machine and baler around a fairly extensive farming district

Chapter Sixteen

Thank goodness William had no knowledge of any of the events back 'home'. No matter how much he hated and despised his parents he would have been devastated to hear of his mother's drowning, accidental or not.

Everything was cruising in the café. The take away meals were very well accepted with patrons travelling long distances to enjoy such gourmet foods. Many of the locals turned up at the café, mainly at the weekends and some were booking numerous tables for functions and parties. One chap was not amused though and he came to see Vanessa one afternoon. The proprietor of the local Fish and Chip shop was furious because his turnover had dropped dramatically due to the takeaway part of the café. He was amazed when he saw the menu boards and the change in methods of operation. William pointed out to the fish and chip man that his business was as far away as it could get within the town boundaries and the café should not have much effect on his business. If it had affected him dramatically maybe he ought to check out his own business first. Maybe he should talk to his customers and find out why they jumped ship and came all this way to get supper. William said, "I have never entered your premises, or tasted your food but you should start there. Is your food inferior to ours? Are your portions as big as ours? Does your menu represent the food that your customers demand? Do you have enough variety? Do you use the best oil available or do you prefer to use the cheapest, and neglect to change it often enough? And most importantly do you supply the very best and freshest fish straight from the markets? The fish man skulked out of the café with a stunned look on his face. He closed down his business the next week and left town.

A few weeks later William suggested to Vanessa that they should call tenders to convert an area adjoining the dining hall to create a semi-alfresco dining area for the summer months. As usual staff problems were a concern but mainly over night. During the day, late afternoon and evenings up to midnight it didn't seem to matter Once the traffic and local trade eased off at night William organised the crew members to prepare and pre-cook, as much of the ingredients as possible. The cold room had been extended to hold the prepared vegetables and other foods and a large freezer added to contain ice cream stocks and some of the extra meats that he bought from time to time to save money.

Talking about staff members; the next problem was to get together a team of outside casuals to work in the garden and adjoining fields. William organised Phillip to pull that one together, with his help, of course. Because there were not so many openings for outside labourers they were more readily available. Both women and men were attracted to this sort of work that needed very little education. The work was mostly casual and often part time meaning married women could fit in some of this whilst running their homes and families.

Most of the work needed very little training just a strong back. Mainly they were employed for planting and harvesting. Of course there were some that weren't prepared to work hard enough to justify the money paid to them so they were quickly eliminated and easily replaced with others who would work well. The outside crew were very easily satisfied due to the lack of this type of work and many of them relished the seasonal work. Often children over the age of twelve were keen to join in, especially students who needed extra income to meet their daily expenses such as bus fares. The result of all this meant that Phillip soon put together a sound reliable team of workers. As in the café the terms, team and teamwork, kept cropping up and even outside in the fields it was obvious that teamwork often made a big difference to the efficiency of the overall output. Phillip was now much better off income wise, so he considered selling off the sheep, which were a lot of work to manage well with only minimal rewards and going in full time with William. With two extra fields under vegetable crops they would be able to supply the local shops instead of the shops supplying the café.

Now that the café and market garden were going well William started to look around the local schools and colleges with a view to finishing his GCE studies and adding other useful subjects. He decided to study only the more relevant subjects for GCE. examinations so he dropped woodwork, Latin, French, and English literature, keeping Mathematics, biology, English language, chemistry and Physics. He added to these Double entry book keeping, Domestic science, accountancy, and business management and typing. He soon realised that he could split up these around the various colleges within the local area. He opted to study some subjects by correspondence to allow him to allocate his time more efficiently. Correspondence courses were much more flexible time wise and would not lock up his daily schedule of having to be at a certain place at a specific time. Chemistry, physics and Domestic science needed physical attendance for laboratory experiments, whereas Mathematics, English, Biology could easily fit into his schedule at home. There was a local college that would allow some early home study in book keeping, accountancy and business management and typing integrated with some classroom sessions. This suited William and he attacked it vigorously. William's grammar school education made the correspondence course easily viable. He could now access details of his scholastic achievements giving him a good start for the future and allowing him to delete the first three years as he continued. For domestic science, William only needed to take a number of tests and examinations to receive the qualifications. The examiners were invited to visit the café where they were served a series of meals, which they declared excellent before scrutinising the kitchen layout, cleanliness and general hygiene procedures. William passed with flying colours and was duly awarded a certificate of merit. All this meant less sessions at the college so he could concentrate on other subjects. Because William could cram in his correspondence studies at any free time he was able to obtain GCE certificates in mathematics, English language and biology in record time to concentrate on business studies.

All these work and learning schedules unfortunately left William with little social interaction with young people of his age. He was well aware of some of the lascivious looks that came his way but was reluctant to take up a steady social life. Fortunately Vanessa was an excellent ballroom dancer in both old time and modern ballroom dancing. She had a very modern radiogram and a good many vinyl records suitable for ballroom dancing. Whenever they were both enjoying some leisure time at home they would crank up the radiogram and Vanessa would teach William the basic steps of the waltz and quick step, Samba, and Foxtrot along with oldies like Gay Gordon, By the time William was ready to indulge in a social life he was quite adept at much of the popular ballroom dance.

One day, out of the blue, so to speak the principal of the college telephoned the farmhouse and asked for William. Vanessa who had answered the call shouted for William, who happened to be in the house at that time, then said, "Here William, Mister Jones the principal of your college wants a word with you."

"Ok Vanessa, I'll Just dry my hands." He replied. When William picked up the receiver he said, "Good morning Mister Jones, this is a pleasant surprise. To what do I owe this unexpected pleasure. What have I done or not done to initiate this call.

"Oh, sorry William, it's nothing like that. We were hoping that you may be able to assist us with some domestic science students. They need much more, 'in the field,' practical experience. Mister Watson was very impressed with your kitchen and menu selection and he was saying that he would love to have a kitchen and staff like yours to assist the students to move on from the classroom setting to a real kitchen, especially a commercial kitchen. Some of our students, as you well know, are aspiring to be professional cooks or chefs. We know how busy you all are at the roadhouse but may it be possible to bring some of our people to spend a little time with you and your staff. Who knows a little bit of it might rub off. We feel sure that they'll benefit greatly if you could oblige."

"Is mister Watson there with you Sir?" William asked.

"Yes William, here he is I'll put him on. Thank you for at least considering our plea William and who knows we might work out a solution.

When Mister Watson picked up the receiver he began with, "Good morning William I take it you are well and the café is thriving as usual. I have been popping in for an evening meal with my wife Audrey from time to time. Although you were not on duty the curries and other foods were excellent. I've been thinking of approaching you with a view to exposing some of my students to commercial cooking. As you are well aware it is a different kettle of fish to domestic and home cooking."

"I have to agree about that and I can assure you, with certain conditions and safeguards, I can assist. I can only cope with about two, maybe four students at a time. I'll trust you to vet them very carefully. I do not, and will not, tolerate time wasters. You must only bring serious students with a cooking career in mind. The College must undertake to have them covered by insurance. I would insist that they come appropriately dressed. No doubt on your visits here you have taken note of my staff's apparel and appearance. Tuesday and Wednesday would suit me. After seven thirty am through to four thirty pm depending on school buses if applicable. That will give them eight hours or so of continuous experience. We will provide disposable gloves and hairnets at our expense. If yourself or another teacher could attend as well they will be more than welcome providing they are prepared to adhere to our dress code, and they might learn a few things whilst they're here"

"Well, William, that's rather a lot to take in at once but you are correct. Those must be the minimum requirements and their parents will have to sign a contract to that effect. Ok that should do for now. I'll arrange to get them to your café as soon as I can and thank you so very much William. Hopefully this can become a permanent arrangement. Thank you and good morning to you."

William turned to Vanessa saying, "I hope you agree with all that, Boss. If we are lucky we might get some aspiring cooks or chefs to come and work with us as permanent employees. Who knows what might eventuate?"

"Well you have committed us to a very intense program William and it all looks very simple. It goes without saying of course, if we are not prepared to teach probable cooks to fill our future needs, who the heck will? Well done I say William. Most of the responsibility and work will land on your shoulders so if you are prepared to accept that and carry it into the future only good can come of it. Thank you and I hope we do not regret any of it."

It was about three weeks or so later before either Vanessa or William heard any more from the college. However, one Monday morning Mister Watson telephoned to have a chat. He assured William that everything was organised ready for the first visit. When did he think would be a suitable day for a trial visit. Much to his surprise William suggested that tomorrow morning would fit in nicely with his schedule. Tuesday being one of the designated days, provided the student end of the equation was up to scratch, William would be ready and waiting for them. He made a thorough check of his store cupboard in anticipation. At the duly appointed time Mister Watson arrived with only two students, shook hands with William and introduced his charges before turning to William and stating, "I think it will be a bit easier if you call me Gregory. Mister Watson is a bit of a mouthful, isn't it."

"Ok Gregory, let's get started, after all time is money. Turning to the students he said ok describe your selves, please. Who are you? Where do you live? And what preparation if any have you had prior to today. Melissa would you like to begin please, then Malcolm can follow. They both began to relax a little as they talked about themselves. They were so tense to begin with. After William took most of that on board he ushered them into the kitchen. "Ok first things first, over to the hand basin and scrub and wash your hands." Both students were a bit surprised and Melissa scrutinised her [what she considered clean hands] but the look that she was receiving from William told her they were not up to scratch, She began to soap up and scrub her skin until it was red raw before showing them to William. Malcolm reluctantly followed suit as William explained that food preparation was as critical as a surgeon preparing for an operation. After all, Cleanliness is next to Godliness. He then gave them each a pair of disposable rubber gloves, which they put on. "Ok, that's the first lesson over. Everything must be scrupulously clean and sterile. All the work benches, pots and pans, utensils. Every item that you are likely to touch including, believe it or not the walls and the floors. There is a scullery outside where we scrub the vegetables before we bring them in. All the potatoes, root vegetables etc need every scrap of dirt removed.

Chapter Seventeen

All of the green leafy vegetables like cauliflowers, cabbages, celery etc, must be thoroughly rinsed to remove any dirt, impurities, insects and damaged leaves.

Apart from being clean you have to minimise cross contamination of foods. So this time your turn Malcolm. What does "cross contamination" mean to you."

"Does it have something to do with germs moving from our hands on to the food and contaminating it making it unsafe to eat?" he replied.

"Good try Malcolm but not quite what I had in mind." Then Melissa burst in. "I think I have heard about this somewhere. Is it something to do with swapping germs from one food type to another type. I think it goes something like, never put raw meat with cooked meat. I think I read somewhere that raw chicken meat can spread salmonella virus to cooked meat. Cooked meats should always be placed on shelves above raw meat never below them."

"Well done Melissa quite correct but only partially so. When you are preparing food and cutting it up on a board, say for salads, it is vital to change or at least thoroughly wash not only the board but also your knives and your hands, change your gloves etc. Never cut up or prepare raw foods such as salads on boards previously used for raw meats" William explained. "So I thought we might bake an apple pie first. Have either of you ever tackled this?

I have plenty of ingredients so I thought we might each prepare and bake a pie of our own. As you can see there is sufficient oven space so there should be no excuses. Melissa, where will you begin, please?"

"Do we need to peel core and slice the apples first? They take quite a long time to soften before including them into the pastry. Do not cook them too long until they go to mush. The pie is much nicer if the apple pieces stay intact."

"Malcolm what next, please?"

"Sift the flour into a suitable bowl and add the shortening, lard and or butter needs to be rubbed into the flour by hand until it resembles bread crumbs, then add ice cold water combine together place in a cool place rest before we roll them out to fit the dishes."

"Yes that sounds ok. Everything we need for the pastry will be in that main pantry by the doorway except for the shortening which is in the cold room next door"

"Ok Malcolm what precautions will you be taking to make sure the pastry comes out A1. We need a crisp golden crust as a basis for all our pies."

"I believe that all the ingredients need to be as cool as possible. The water needs to be iced and even the surface used for working. The dough has to be soft, light and airy and rolling should be on a cold surface. Some cooks like to roll the pastry with a wine bottle filled with iced water. That's why good cooks use marble or stone slabs if possible. All three of them worked separately and soon all the pastries had been rested then rolled out then they were fitted to the dishes"

"Meanwhile the Bramley seedling apples had cooled ready to be included in the pastry shells. Then on with the lid, roll or pinch the edges to seal them and make a couple of slits in the top to let the steam out. My Mum likes to cut up some of the left over pastry to decorate the top." Said Melissa.

All three pies were cooked to perfection as William accustomed his helpers to the thermostats and length of cooking using his ovens which were familiar to him. When carefully taken from the oven they were a joy to see.

"Well done the both of you now another question. What does your mother dread the most when baking a meal?"

Melissa answered first with a snap decision, "Yorkshire puddings. They seldom come out the way they should. Either they are soft and soggy or flat lumps of dough in the bottom of the pan."

"Ok Melissa that will never happen again I promise you. And you Malcolm your worst nightmare or at least your Mum's that is"

"Mum has tried and tried but she cannot

bake a decent sponge cake. They always end up soggy, out of shape and stodgy."

"Okay we'll come back to sponge cakes. For now we'll concentrate on the dreaded Yorkshire puddings. Any ideas how to get a perfect, Yorkshire pudding, every time, without fail. Someone important is coming to dinner. The puddings must be perfect or else?"

Melissa said," Mum reckons it's the oven that's no good. Sometimes she says the flour is too old. The co-op must have sold her old stale flour. Anyway, whatever, they never come out right.

Malcolm said "That's what my mother says as well. Sometimes she reckons it might be the thundery weather that makes them flop."

"Okay we'll each make Yorkshire puddings. There are one or two misconceptions but generally it is wrong procedure that causes them to flop. They should never come out soft and soggy. That is the sign of a bad cook. Oven type such as Gas, electric or open fire should not matter. What is most important is temperature. The batter is important. The flour should be as fresh as possible. Make up the batter as per the book. This is important but need not be too exact. Beat the batter well to include as much air as possible. Some cooks and some cook books are adamant the batter should be prepared well before hand and left to stand. I was led to believe that it's not important. One trick that I was shown is when the oven is ready sprinkle a little fresh flour over the batter and stir it in, works every time but do not beat it again just stir the flour in lightly. Get the oven searing hot. If you are using an open fire chuck a heap of extra wood on to get a good blaze. Add a decent amount of beef dripping to the cooking pans, place the cooking pans in the oven until they are very hot. Take out the pans and tip the hot fat from one to the other pan and discard any excess. Do not place the pans on a cold surface. Place them on a trivet or cooling rack then working quickly pour the batter equally into the dishes then put them back into the oven. The fat in the pans should be hot enough to begin the cooking even before they go back into the oven. Close the oven door and leave it closed until the puddings have risen to their full height and are nice and crisp. When ready just add good beef gravy or golden syrup." Because we hadn't prepared a hot roast dinner to go with the Yorkshire puddings we served them with a good dressing of either maple or golden syrup according to taste. They were delicious, nice and crisp and crunchy. The students were amazed how easy it was. After their impromptu meal we went through the procedure to prepare and cook the perfect sponge cake. Gregory Watson who had hardly said a word, came back into the kitchen, shook hands with William and asked about their next session. "Before you leave I have some homework or prep-work for you to consider before we meet again. I want you both to work out some recipes for the future. You have had a good look at my menu boards. These menus are designed to provide good wholesome meals at relatively low cost and they are the sort of meals that we can have on tap in case we get a rush on and have to feed, say a coach load of people quickly. The food needs to be nutritious, filling and tasty. What I want you to do is look at my boards see if you can interpret the contents.

Then go home and write up a recipe for a tasty soup, a casserole and a hearty meat stew. You have both had a good look around my stocks, but don't necessarily stick to those, use your initiative. I need you to have a quick look into the cold room and freezers to check the meat stocks and please note the large quantity of bones in stock especially a couple of ham bones. I have an arrangement with my butcher whereby I buy plenty of good meaty bones which we use regularly in abundance. Thank you for your attendance, I hope you have learned quite a lot today, good afternoon."

Melissa spoke up saying 'Thankyou Chef for all your help today and we will attack your dedicated tasks with a lot of vigour. Thank you again, until next time. I hope I can come again tomorrow. I've loved today's class"

William left the arrangements to Gregory to decide who came and when. William was looking forward to reading and discussing the menus both his and theirs, it should make for an interesting morning. He was particularly looking forward to see how much of the environment in the café they have managed to absorb. Of course it remained to be seen who Gregory would bring tomorrow. William was certain these two would return but not exactly when. He was particularly impressed with Melissa who would certainly make a good cook.

The next day Gregory turned up with the same two students, Melissa and Malcolm. William set some simple tasks to keep them busy whilst he studied their recipes, made notes and suggestions for improvements. They had both coped extremely well but Melissa shone through as being much more suitable. She had obviously spent quite some time in their family kitchen and her Grandmother's kitchen. She lacked in knowledge of, and use of herbs in recipes but that would come. Also some of the essentials, or at least what he considered were essentials, were not included. When William had read and criticised the recipes he handed them back to the students to appraise. By the time they had both read their own and each other's work it was time to sit down for a cup of tea and scones whilst they discussed the recipes and his comments. He took them through into the café where they could sit down at a quiet corner table to relax and chat. Both of their submissions were very thoughtfully presented as he had expected and would have sufficed as they were written but he suggested, rather than insisted, certain improvements. He firstly told them that the tastes would be greatly enhanced if they had sealed the bones in a hot pan with a little fat. He said that the easiest way to do that was, if they had one, to use a heavy bottomed saucepan and fry the bones over a hot gas turning frequently until every surface was sealed. The same pan could then be used for the soup by adding prepared vegetables herbs and spices. He told them that using fresh herbs was infinitely better than dried ones. Just tie the stems together with a piece of string, drop them in on the top and remove them later with the bones.

They returned to the kitchen all fired up and ready to go. William said, "Okay you cooks, the kitchen is yours for the day. I need you both to put together a suitable recipe and produce a nice tasty soup for six diners and a second course of your choice. Please remember this is a commercial kitchen and there will be others working around you. They have menus to prepare and serve for our customers so must have priority, within reason, so go to it and good luck. There is always an element of luck in any kitchen, no matter how competent the staff. Things do go haywire, food does get thrown out, for various reasons, Myself and other members of staff will help you locate ingredients, tools and utensils. We can help with gas levels and temperature controls only. Please feel free to make notes of anything that you wish to discuss later, such as tastes and flavours, how to achieve them, what, if any, herbs and spices may have improved the result. Thank you for your time now it is up to you."

Everyone was very impressed with the culinary skills of both students. Both of their soups were tasty and wholesome, although as William had expected Melissa had included something that was not mentioned in any cook book he had ever read, 'love and devotion'. These are essential ingredient in any recipe, and have the capacity to lift a meal to great heights, often way above any reasonable expectations.

On top of an excellent soup she had taken a dish from the storeroom and served one serve of soup into the heated dish and presented it on the dish with a decent dollop of cream on the top and a nice arrangement of parsley sprigs around it.

Anyway, we move on to the second course. Malcolm wanted to prepare a curry for seconds but William steered him away from that because of the need to steep the meat and spices over night, so he produced a very tasty, succulent stew with plenty of meat and vegetables. The result was near excellent because he had added a garnish of fresh herbs to finish it off after serving it up on a deep dish.

As he might have expected Melissa had gone all out to impress. Whilst trying to imitate photographs in an American magazine she had swallowed the bullet, so to speak. She had undertaken a very serious challenge to produce something very artistic as well as wholesome and nutritious. She had only seen the photographs in magazines but if the Americans could do it so could she. Firstly she needed a base to assemble the ingredients onto so she borrowed William's new bike, which she rode somewhat precariously down to the bakers shop where she managed to obtain special barbeque rolls which should do nicely. Back at the café she flattened out some of the special sausage meat from the cold room into thick circular slabs slightly larger than the size of the buns. She rolled them out more than half an inch thick and fried them on a very hot plate. They were already quite spicy she thought as she tasted a little of the raw mince meat then some of the cooked mince meat. The next ingredient was a thick slice of cheddar cheese carefully cut from the big block in the pantry. There was a packet of cheese slices in there ready to go but Melissa bypassed those as somewhat inferior to the real thing. She made up a tasty sauce from tomato ketchup, hp sauce, and Kraft salad cream which she spread over the cheese.

Now it was down to the nitty gritty, the all important assembly and presentation. The rolls were cut carefully in half and toasted on the cut side only. Next the cheese, which was quickly warmed through but not melted.

The hot 'Hamburger' sat on top of the cheese followed by slices of pickled beetroot, lettuce, white salad onion slices and thin slivers of celery and raw carrots. Unfortunately this was not the best time of the year for salads as tomatoes and cucumber were out of season and very expensive. The dish needed very little seasoning thanks to the highly seasoned sausage meat and the sauces. William was watching carefully and with great anticipation, what would happen next. The burger really was special. It looked extremely good, very artistic and mouth watering but how could Melissa present and serve such a meal. The burger was much too tall to fit into any body's mouth even if they worked out how to get it up there. Not to worry Melissa had it all covered. In the pantry she had located some special, extra long, thin skewers labelled 'Satay sticks'. She firmly planted one of these vertically through the middle of the burger pushing it right through to the plate. The burger was served on a dinner sized plate with an assortment of fresh herbs scattered around the base. She added a sizeable dollop of her special sauce on one side, a dollop of the Kraft salad cream alongside of that and a dollop of Tomato Ketchup at the other side. A serrated steak knife and a fork lying on one side completed the picture, and what a picture it was. It had become obvious that this burger was meant to be eaten with a knife and fork, rather than take-away style in the hands.

Everyone was amazed and eager to try a generous slice declaring it a culinary masterpiece. Melissa's soup had set them up for something special and Malcolm's meal was excellent but different. His was a roadhouse special, which was what could be expected in a setting like this. Melissa's on the other hand was a special, top of the range restaurant experience. Both meals were a special surprise to everyone present. Gregory Watson was absolutely flabbergasted. Never in his wildest dreams could he have expected an outcome like this.

He and William needed to get together for a conference of war. Where could they go next. William suggested a meeting without the students maybe over a meal to decide where to go. Gregory believed that these two were well ahead of expectations and with a little assistance would go far. He felt they were already beyond his capacity to teach them anymore. William suggested that he and Gregory get together with Melissa's parents then with Malcolm's parents to work out the next step. Knowing that the town, and the café in particular, were both short of capable, proficient cooks so he was suggesting some type of apprenticeships or cadetships attached to the roadhouse café. Both students were of a suitable age to leave school and enter into the workforce. William could absorb them both into his staff and Gregory could arrange to get them certified in their chosen careers. The café could then continue to indulge the training classes with Gregory's involvement as this one had.

William firstly arranged a meeting with Melissa's parents. He asked Melissa to talk to her family members including her Grandmother. She and she alone could decide if commercial cooking would be the correct career path for her. Before any get together was organised

William had a long chat with Melissa, letting her know that he was very happy to have her on his team if that's what she wanted He pointed out that even in more conventional establishments like hotels and restaurants the working hours could and in fact would be horrendous and at times unbelievably hectic, as well as broken shifts. Everyone wanted to dine at the same time, be it breakfast, lunch or dinner. Here at the roadhouse it was mainly much easier except when coaches turned up out of the blue. The move into more conventional meals like soups and stews was designed to smooth out the flow. It was possible to put good meals on the table very quickly where as 'a-la-carte' was very time consuming and travelling public didn't have the time to spare. Lorries never arrived in convoys nor yet did cars and other road users. Weekends did get a bit hectic especially now that they were catering more for the local trade rather than just travellers. He understood her love of cooking and her possible desire to make a career out of it, but, commercial cooking was so different to home baking.

The meeting with Melissa's parents and

Grandmother went off very pleasantly. None of the family members had ever been to the roadhouse, not even for fuel they lived a longish bike ride out of town but there was a reasonable bus service. Working twelve hour shifts was a bit hard but it minimised the amount of travelling. The outcome of it all was that Melissa was offered a full time job as assistant cook with a possible upgrade to cook when she turned eighteen. She was expected to rotate among the other cooks to cover every day.

Malcolm and his family also attended a meal-cum-meeting event at the roadhouse. His family, especially his father were not really enthusiastic about his possible career but eventually agreed to give it a chance. No better work chances had shown up and any job was better than no job. The penalty rates and overtime availability made his choice more acceptable. The family lived within the township but at the other end. Malcolm owned a roadworthy bicycle and except in bad weather it was a pleasant ride to get to work every day. William gave him the position of assistant cook also with a promise of upgrade on his eighteenth birthday. These two appointments seriously removed much of William's work load as both parties settled in well with only a minimum of supervision.

Although the titles meant very little they gave the two young people a lift in stature which would help them amalgamate their skills experience and abilities as well as a little more salary. They both had a long way to go but William was certain that both would become useful members of his staff. Quite a lot of the work involved simple everyday roadhouse menus and not a great deal of A-La-Carte full menu cooking.

The cooking school was going extremely well partly because Gregory was doing a great job of selecting students who genuinely wanted to become qualified cooks and maybe qualified chefs. The exemplary examples set by Melissa and Malcolm gave the new students a serious goal to aim at. They could see that this could lead to a very worthwhile career if they stuck to it.

Talking about careers set William on a new path. Although he was travelling extra well he felt that there had to be more. It was good being called a chef but he thought he might like to be a real chef one day. Unfortunately his present occupations and silly shifts did not allow him any chance of training under a qualified chef. One afternoon whilst cogitating over coffee and more of Vanessa smashing scones he came up with a possible solution.

William contacted Gregory at the college and invited him for lunch. Gregory was eager to attend any meal when William was cooking. Over a sumptuous luncheon William posed a question. He needed to qualify to be a real chef. Did Gregory or the college have details of course of tuition and a list of skills needed to become a real chef. Gregory was sure that he could help with the information but he didn't have the necessary skills to teach William. He later produced a curriculum for the course, but not through the local college. He and William went through the curriculum carefully and worked out a few ideas. One of the basic requirements was the necessary skills to break down animal carcasses from one big lump of meat and bone into chops and steaks. He needed to know what different steak, cuts were called, where they came from on a body and how to extract them efficiently with a minimum of waste. He also had to know how to cook and present them to his customers. He also had to know about beef classification and quality. The same applied to Pork bodies, lamb bodies as well as mutton bodies he would be expected to be able to classify them within a reasonable margin. William was getting quite despondent about becoming a qualified chef until he came up with a great idea, he hoped, anyway. He remembered, whilst chatting to Michael at the butcher's shop that he had been told that Michael was in fact a fully qualified butcher and had trained in a highly prestigious wholesale abattoir and butchery.

William hopped on his bike and rode around to the butcher's shop. He found Michael behind the counter where he was serving a customer. His apprentice was out at the rear of the shop chopping up lumps of beef to fit into the mincer.

When Michael was free and no other customers in sight he came out to the work area saying, "Now then William this is a surprise.

Have you killed off all your customers with that God-awful curry or one of your soups?"

"Now, now, Michael stop blithering on and make us all a cup of your rotten instant coffee whilst I tell you a funny story, and think on, every item of food that we put on the table in our premises is thoroughly laced with chunks of meat from this very shop. I have lowered myself to come and visit your premises during the day when there are plenty of witnesses around to observe me and report me to the local gossip mongers. As you well know I usually sneak in the rear door very early in the mornings before the gossips are about. I have decided that this one horse town, if there is still one around, 'horse that is', that you haven't turned into sausages yet, needs a half decent butcher who knows what he is doing. I was hoping you just might educate me to the same heights as yourself. Ok I realise it will be extortionately expensive but I am willing to tolerate that situation to achieve my latest goals. What do you say about that?"7

"Oh my goodness William you get more and more verbose by the day and you always had too much to say. Damn that girl Vanessa, she has turned my peaceful, happy, existence into a maelstrom since she brought you into our lovely town. So now enough of your bullshit 'boy' why are you round here in my shop at this time of day."

"Actually I came around here to ask you for a favour but I realise now that I came to the wrong establishment. You see Michael, I have decided to become a qualified chef, and the powers that be, tell me I need certain qualifications to make that possible. I do not have any avenues of time at my disposal to spend hours and hours with a qualified chef in a hotel or upmarket restaurant to learn a few tricks of the trade, as you know. Gregory Watson at the college kindly looked into the problem for me and obtained a suitable curriculum for me to work by. The most outstanding requirement, is to become a butcher of sorts. I need to be able to name all the bits of a body of beef, know where they fit and how to separate them from the rest of the carcass with a minimum of waste. I also have to know how to classify a good beef body from a poor beef body. Michael, not withstanding all that claptrap the same applies to a pork body and a sheep body. When I say sheep I include lambs, hoggets and adult sheep. Of course I don't expect an answer immediately as I realise it will take you a day or two to assimilate all that information and make sense of any of it. Michael, I am at your mercy. You are my best chance of doing this successfully, so please be nice to me in my delicate position."

"I have taken all that on board William and freely interpolating it all. I am assuming that you wish to spend a good many countless hours in our company, annoying shit out of us, messing up our daily schedules, and getting in our way. You certainly haven't left me much choice. I either have to share my limited knowledge with you or listen to any more of this rubbish." Turning quickly to his apprentice he said, "And you can take that ridiculous grin off your ugly mush before I cut it off with my cleaver. Ok William I know I am going to regret this, but I'll do it just for you, but the first time you give me any more of this crap you will be banned for life, "Once you get your arse into gear and are ready to learn something just let me know. You've done so much to improve my business by changing your business, how could I refuse and we might even enjoy your company, so long as you keep your big gob shut most of the time." William shook hands with Michael commenting, "Well that's a great relief Michael. I was thinking I might have to find another butcher but I would miss our daily wrangles. As you know I am a busy boy so I will stick my head in any time I have some time. I would especially like to be here every morning when you start breaking down the beef bodies even though I won't always be able to stay all day if we get too busy at the roadhouse. Who knows Michael you might even learn bit more than me by the time I'm finished."

"Thank God for small mercy's. Who the hell would put up with you all day?" retorted Michael, "So now bugger off we have work to do before we can knock off tonight. We have lost enough time already."

On his way back to the roadhouse William called into the public library to scour the joint for any books they may have on butchering that he could study at home and begin to familiarise himself with the various terms and cuts of meat. He put in a quick call to Gregory to see if he could supply any text books or maybe supply details of people who could. Gregory was very optimistic and he had already been working towards that end with some success.

William arrived at the butcher's premises before him the next morning and was sitting on a low wall in the back yard. He had outfitted himself with a set of white clothes and he was raring to get started.

William's first comment was, "Good afternoon Michael. Thank you for making the effort to come along and help."

"And you can go and get stuffed you rotten little shit stirrer. I suppose you've been up all night so all you had to do was hop on that crazy velocipede of yours and race off down here. I hope you don't still stink of curry."

No, wrong again mate. The kitchen was extremely busy until about midnight the everything seemed to stop so I bailed out, quick smart, time for a hot shower and crash into bed for a few hours kip. Forgot to set the alarm of course but still got out in reasonable time for a hot shower then onto the old velocipede for a quick spot check at the café but all was well. They didn't need my input so I told them where to find me if needed and hot footed it around here to get you off your arse before the delivery truck arrives with another load of seconds and sweepings up at the abattoir. A bit of sawdust off the floor helps to bulk out the minces."

"Hey! Pal. It's far too early in the day for your snide remarks even if they are true. If you want to do this course, get off my back at least until lunchtime, Ok."

"Right you are there mate, I just needed a quick reality check to make sure your brain is still working. So what do you need me to tackle first or do I just watch the master at work."

"The truck is due as you guessed so we need to drain that steriliser bath and pull out all those hooks and dry them off and fit them up here onto the overhead rail. As the bodies are unloaded we have to hang them up and roll them into the cool room. One serious point, pal, is make sure that the different types of bodies do not touch other types. Lamb carcasses must not touch pork carcasses etc. If you change from pork say to beef or vice versa remember to change your gloves."

"Yes Michael I understand. At our end we refer to it, as cross contamination

Especially with chicken, because of the risk of salmonella poisoning."

Here we go pal get those doors open and grab a body or two. Maybe if you take the lamb bodies first then the pork. I'll make a start on the beef. There will be a couple of bacon bodies in here as well so I'll give you a hand with those.

Once all the bodies were hanging in the cool room they made a start on breaking them down. William was eager to start on the beef but Michael had to forestall him. He pointed out that they were in dire need to stock the shop with both lamb and pork initially so the bodies were halved and the work began. They concentrated on removing the best cuts such as legs and loins, bypassing the rest for the apprentice to sort out and mince. The shop soon looked good with various joints dangling from the rails. They continued breaking the smaller bodies until the young bloke arrived. His first task of the day was to organise morning tea. It began with a quick trip along the street to the bakers shop to collect some nice fresh buns to go with the rest of the ingredients, which Michael kept in the shop. They sat down in the back room but kept an eye on the shop door, although it was still early. When the first customer came into the shop Michael sent William out to serve her, mainly to observe his technique and limited knowledge. William pulled off his gloves before entering the shop and pulled on a clean pair. The ladies needs were very straight forward and William only needed help with the till and pricing. "Well done pal, I can almost see a butcher in that skinny hide of yours, but you really need to brighten up your act on the money side if you're going to make the grade. Get the brass, [money] out of them as quick as you can and slam it in the till where it's safe."

William was designated pork and lamb butcher for the rest of the day whilst Michael concentrated in extracting the better cuts off the beef carcass until lunch time. After lunch they had a big clean up then set about getting the bacon and ham separated ready for salting. Each piece was carefully trimmed and tidied up then immersed in a special brine solution to cure for a few days. By the time that the bacon pig had been dealt with William realised that butchering was quite hard yakka. It used Different muscle groups to his own work, although the mixture of café and market gardening should have kept him ultra fit anyway. At the end of day one, William shook hands with Michael and thanked him

"William that was a great day in spite of your witticisms," remarked Michael I enjoyed our day and we achieved a ton of work. If I had been on my own I would have had to leave the bacon pig until tomorrow and I really need to get more bacon and ham cured ready to use. I am a full day ahead and that's great, pal. You know what, I might have actually learned a few tricks today as well as you. When are you likely to come again."

"Not before tomorrow. I will have to assess the situation at cafe and garden before I know for sure. Phillip is doing a fantastic job with the market garden."

Chapter Eighteen

Whilst William was sorting out his students Maude and Penny were getting accustomed to their new surroundings both at home and at work. Maude was starting from scratch in her offices. There was no starting point so she relied heavily on Penny's support to set up an office structure that would work for both of them with minimum of drama. They hadn't started any juniors yet so there was just the two of them. Even the General Manager seldom showed his face deciding that it was best left to the girls to lay out the furniture and filing cabinets.

Back at their new home everything was rosy. Neither of the girls had ever lived in this sort of luxury. Almost waited on hand and foot with gallons of hot water, heated rooms and real comfort. There was always a supply of cakes tarts and biscuits on hand. Penny was watching Maude guzzling her way through a mountain of sweet delights one evening when she commented. "We'll have to speak to Alison, Maude. We can't eat all these cakes. We will both get as fat as pigs at this rate."

"Heck who's complaining. Keep them coming I say. I am really enjoying being spoilt like this." Replied Maude.

Why don't you shut your face Maude. It's alright for you, you're as skinny as a rail, straight up and down, where as I've always had to wrestle with my weight. All my life I have been tubby and this is catastrophic "

"What's with you tonight? Where did all that come from Penny?" Asked Maude, "You don't have to eat any of the cakes at all. Are we having our first argument Penny. Don't let's spoil our new home this early please. You are right, of course but I don't have to eat the cakes in front of you if it bothers you. I can take mine up to my room later. In the morning I'll ask Alison to be a bit more circumspect with her cooking. She should be able to cut out the richer fare and reduce the total amount as well. We might have to think about early morning or evening walks around the streets, that should help. There's plenty of nice scenery around here. I was sitting up in bed last night thinking about how Dad is getting on but I daren't get in touch with him. He'll just have to stew in his own juices. I just wish that I knew someone who is familiar with him and could let me know how he is going"

"Yea well if you did know someone like that one of you would eventually slip up, and he could find out where you're living and neither of us want that. He's a big boy now so let him sort it out himself. Did you check up with your old workmates to see if he had been in touch with them?"

"Yes, there is only Maureen from your old office that I was ready to contact. She said that my dad had tried to get some information on our whereabouts but nobody could help.

The new offices were ready to go now and in fact next Monday the rest of the staff will be on hand as the factory cranks up into gear. That will mean staff rosters to arrange and type up. Lists of names, and personal details, of all the workers, to be entered into the files. Wages list to be typed up. There will be endless meetings to be minuted, and typed up ready to be circulated.

'D' Day finally arrived in the office. Maude and Penny strode purposely along the street with a brisk breeze in their faces. Today would soon tell them whether they had got everything set up correctly and efficiently ready for the onslaught. As they entered the office and removed their coats, Maude said, "You'd better put the kettle on straight away. We need to get some coffee on the go early as we might not get time later, Penny. I'll switch on the telex machine etc, so we'll be ready when they come in. Let's hope our assistants arrive a bit early as they will be on deck immediately or sooner."

Hardly had Maude finished speaking when the door burst open as two young ladies tried to enter at the same time. Oh well that's seems like a good start but would it continue. Maude took Margaret under her wing to get started whilst Penelope took Audrey to her desk. Introductions were made and the day had begun. The personal details were entered into the appropriate files then the girls were shown to their desks to begin learning the ritual required. Both girls seemed keen to learn and understand the procedure, make themselves useful, and fit in. First and most importantly they were shown through to the little amenities room where they had to learn how to work the coffee machine. Very soon they were all flat out dealing with the first day's events. They had little time to chat during the day and they were both so glad to lock up the office before the brisk walk home and a lovely hot shower. Neither of them had even stopped for lunch. They had taken sandwiches from home and of course some of those marvellous cakes.

Because both of their bedrooms had en-suite showers they could both indulge at the same time and, Oh boy, was it a great feeling. Having spent most of her young life with only a begrudging bath on Friday evenings and since they moved she had only managed to have an occasional bath when she stayed over at Dora's place. If ever Maude had been asked to define luxury she would definitely have said, "Please, an en-suite shower with unlimited hot water."

She could feel the heat washing away the stressful day at work. What a joy it would have been to indulge in something like this on those bad days when things went awfully wrong at her previous employment. Both of the two new girls had conducted themselves well but they had a lot to learn.

By the week's end they were beginning to meld together into an efficient team. This was a new experience for Maude, stepping up from a reception desk to be an office manager was big time. It was a position that she had little experience of except during the odd bouts of sickness when her immediate boss had flue and other illness from time to time and during her summer holidays. She would need to rule with a firm hand initially then maybe relaxing a little once the office was more settled and everyone knew their job and their places. Maude had waited a long time for either of these privileges and to receive both of them at the same time, especially after the horrors of living with her family after Billy disappeared. Oh, how she would love to know where Billy was, and if he was doing ok. The only solace in that direction was the papers issued by the County Court in Worcester. Billy must surely have landed on his feet but how the devil had he got all that way without anyone knowing anything about it. If Billy had not been well set up surely the court would have vetoed the adoption and name change.

Chapter Nineteen

At about this time Vanessa made a serious commitment to the business by deciding to accept William's idea of the alfresco dining area. She wrote to the town council for permission to go ahead and was granted provisional approval subject to the plans, when drafted, being appropriate for the area. The town was in need of more job opportunities and because Vanessa had already demonstrated that she could manage that now that the market garden was shaping up well. The local ladies benefited most from the possibilities of working between school hours to earn extra income whilst the family was at school. Phillip actually had a healthy waiting list of potential employees ready to fit in part time.

Vanessa was keen to meet the town engineer. He had promised to be at the café early but time was getting on and she had just completed a twelve-hour shift at the desk. She was about to leave and head off home when he finally arrived full of apologies for his lateness. Vanessa called William out to join her and he brought the architects plans with him. The engineer was quite amazed. Most people only produced a rough pencil sketch or just relied on word of mouth. Architects don't come cheap so most people rely on mere basics to save money in case the ideas didn't even begin to make it to the next stage. William and Vanessa had decided to do this correctly to save any problems later. The Architect had carefully drawn up the plans and including all the utility details as well. The council engineer realised that most of his work had already been attended to. All the measurements, power needs, gas lines, hot and cold water lines outlets and of course drains were all there ready. It only needed a quick check over for any possible errors and his stamp and signature of approval. They all three sat down at one of the tables and Vanessa signalled the waitress to bring them refreshments. It's quite amazing how quickly a mug of tea or coffee along with a plateful of fresh scones with jam and cream can improve the atmosphere. The engineer told them he was glad they had picked the best Architect in the district. He had worked with their chosen expert a number of times and admitted that he did not come cheap but he was worth every penny they paid him. Once the plans were drawn up and checked there would never be any unforseen, problems neither with the buildings nor the utilities. He would see it through to the end ready for furniture. William was able to leave all that to Vanessa whilst he and Phillip sorted out the hothouses. They found a local painter to remove the flaky paint and reprime and repaint the woodwork. They soon found out that the easiest method of attack was to start at one end and remove the lines of panes from top to bottom repaint the wood and reset the panes with new putty. The weather did not help but the job was progressing well, so well in fact that it would be as good as a new building when completed.

During the painting episode Phillip and his crew assembled and mixed the high quality soil that was needed for a good crop. Meanwhile William and a tough band of helpers began to remove all the glass from the new greenhouse. They had hired a good stack of strong pallets. The glass was thicker than expected, therefore heavier. The painter moved backwards and forwards between the two sights with a view to having the framework ready for the glass to be replaced as soon as the framework was reinstalled against the wall on the new sight. The farmer had a large flattop trailer, which he was glad to lend to William along with an old, fairly decrepit fork lift. William soon realised the potential of the fork lift because they could enter the building through the double doors at one end with a pallet sitting on the forks which they lifted up close to the framework to receive the glass as it came loose thus saving many hours of backbreaking toil and greatly reducing the possibility of breaking any glass or better still hurting anyone. The painter was also able to stand on the palette to do his work. He located a special palette with a flat plywood surface with no gaps. He had plenty of room on the palette for all his tools and tins of paint. In much less time than expected the woodwork was renovated, reprimed and painted.

Once the glass was removed it was taken to the new sight ready to be reinstalled. The framework was then quickly finished ready for dismantling. The panels were obviously designed to be transported on ordinary trailers with a certain amount of care. The glass walls were designed to sit on top of 3 ft high brick walls so the local builder was contacted to lay heavy foundations and build the walls. Being able to pre-measure the building at the farm made the work more accurate so it fitted exactly. The main part of the frame was bolted together. They had soaked the threads in penetrine to try and soften any rust. Most of the bolts unscrewed reasonably easily although a few were difficult. The frame sections had to be tied loosely together as the bolts came out then they were separated and lowered to the ground each adjoining pair were carefully numbered to make sure they fitted back neatly together. Each panel was slightly more than 8 ft wide but as they didn't have far to go they were not too much of a problem. Once the mortar in the new brick wall was hard enough reassembly began. The first section had a wall with double doors at both ends. Once bolted to the brick walls the paint was retouched prior to reglazing. It was easier to position the second frame now they had the other one for support.

Whilst all this was going on the old greenhouse was reprimed, repainted and the glass refitted in new putty. This building would surely last for many years to come. When William finally caught up with his Boss she was happy to report that the annex was completed except for painting. Vanessa could now buy and organise delivery of the furniture ready for the Grand Opening. William was putting together a very special menu in preparation for the big day. If only half the people turned up as promised it would be chaotic. Thank goodness for William's instant meals, which had now proved themselves well. They would be able to feed a good many people quite quickly.

At last both the greenhouse and the annex were finished the same week. That weekend would be celebration day. Important guests and friends had official invitations to dine in style whilst the rest of the mob and a huge gathering it was were feted with Takeaway meals. There were huge vats of soups stews and curries but most favoured of all was a massive sausage sizzle. William had scoured his suppliers and obtained Barbeque hot plates to roast large quantities of Michael's sausages, tons of sliced onions, buckets of tomato ketchup and bottles of mustard. These delights were snuggled into special hotdog buns from Peter who had been madly baking day and night. The kids particularly loved them. Buckets of soup were served in take-away mugs [no washing up]. The party went on until very late and by then the crew were absolutely knackered.

William and Vanessa decided not to charge a set fee for the night. They set up honour buckets around the Greenhouse site and at the roadhouse with a message that read

WE HOPE YOU HAVE ALL ENJOYED
YOURSELVES.ALL DONATIONS TO
ASSIST WITH COSTS GRATEFULLY
RECEIVED WITH OUR THANKS

Vanessa and William
And All Our Suppliers

There was a staggering amount of cash and even a good many cheques donated that evening. Even some of the ingredients were donated as well. Advertising placards around both venues congratulated everyone, especially, Michael, Peter, Ernie, the Co-op, and many other suppliers of tomato sauce, coca cola, cool drinks, tea coffee, Milo, Cadbury's cocoa. Some of the suppliers such as coca cola sent a team of sales staff along with lots of free samples, placards, prizes and give-aways. The suppliers love this type of venue because of the large local trade and through vehicle trade as well. Some of them had designed suitable signage for the celebration and for the continued business still to come.

The outcome was so gratifying to them all on both sides of the fence. Most of the council members attended, some for the first time ever. Tomorrow morning they were all dreading. The mighty party had produced a great amount of debris They arrived a little tardily after a restless night only to find that the big clean up was already under way. Many local people had turned out with pick-up trucks, tipping lorries, provided free of charge by the council, vans and even a horse and cart. There were lots of kids dashing about hoping to find some hidden goodies.

Chapter Twenty

Phillip and his team had a busy week ahead of them. All the soil mix had to be barrowed into the greenhouse raked and settled down. Overhead wires needed to be arranged over each row of plants and string droppers attached to support the tomato plants. Then of course the actual planting and watering of the crop. It took most of the week but it all went well. Once the team knew what was expected William and Phillip climbed over the wall to inspect the new greenhouse and the crops. The greenhouse was finished with the first half ready for planting. The second half was ready for soil as soon as some of the crew members were free. They were given the massive job of collecting and mixing the next lot of soil mix for the new greenhouse.

The planter from Holland had arrived and

been deployed to plant a crop of greens such as cabbage, cauliflower and sprouts. The planting attachment worked well and saved a lot of time. The machine was converted back to plant potatoes, which were growing well at the moment. William had been studying a seed planter that also planted two rows of seeds like beetroot carrots parsnips, onions, turnips and Swedes. It was a very simple machine that separated the seeds and planted them at the correct spacing in the rows thus saving much labour and much seed. It also reduced singling with a hoe to prevent overcrowding. The firm in Holland who supplied the big planter was waiting for new supplies to arrive from America. William ordered three of them to fit on a homemade toolbar to hook on to the three-point attachment on the Ferguson tractor. When they arrived they would be able to plant 6 rows nice and neatly at the same time. Phillip said that once his current crop of lambs could be weaned in the early autumn he would begin ploughing up the other two fields ready for next spring planting. He was getting very excited with this new type of farming especially the greenhouse crops. Because the roadhouse would absorb much of the produce there would be no problems with poor markets and low prices. The new machinery from Holland was looking very exciting and he was keen to try it out and now that the rows would be evenly spaced they would be able to utilise a new type of weed hoeing machinery to fit the Ferguson. In the olden days farmers used a scruffler towed with a cart horse to remove the weeds between the rows of crops. Great though these machine were it was impossible to keep them travelling straight so the tines needed to be far enough apart not to damage the crop The new type steerage hoes fitted onto the three point linkage of the Ferguson and had an operator on a seat on the machine who could move the tines sideways by turning a type of steering wheel. All this, meant they removed the weeds up closer to the plants so reducing hand hoeing costs.

As soon as the lambs were weaned and separated from the ewes the ewes were taken to market. The lambs stayed in the fields until they settled down to feed on grass and oats.

When autumn weather stopped the grass growing the lambs were sold off to a local farmer who was very pleased with their size and quality. A few days later, Phillip organised one of his men who'd had plenty of ploughing experience, to set up the Ferguson tractor and the mouldboard plough. It was only a single furrow but the ground was very tough due to years of grazing. The tractor used most of its available power to work the plough but the result was excellent. After a few good frosts to break it down the rotary hoe would soon turn it into a lovely fine tilth ready for sowing the seeds.

The tomato crop had yielded well and was either sold at the front desk or used in the kitchen. There were quite a lot of tomatoes that were too late to ripen properly so William had a small team of workers go in and pick any that were left which he cooked up with a heap of onions and spices to make a tasty green tomato chutney. Much of the chutney was used to spice up the menus in the kitchen but a good many jars were sold on the front counter of the café. Phillip got a crew to remove the plant residue burn the straw to kill any fungus on it then removed the string hangars, which would be replaced with new ones in the following spring. The spent soil was dug out and replaced with new mixes ready to be replanted. Early next spring the whole greenhouse would be closed up and fumigated to remove any insect pests before the whole scenario began again. After the next tomato season Phillip and William were intending to experiment with indoor flowering plants for sale in the café but for this year it would only be used to sprout the new seasons seed potatoes and sow seeds of greens ready for planting in the spring. They managed to obtain supplies of tomato seeds from France so they could grow their own plants for the greenhouses. They would need more than 500 good strong plants. Quite large quantities of green vegetable seed were acquired from the best seed houses and duly planted in early spring along with lots and lot of onions, carrots turnips and Swedes. The onions were needed on a daily basis for the café, and of course they stored well for later use. They used white onions for salads etc because of their milder taste and brown onions for cooking. One supplier sent a large container of red Spanish onion seeds at half price because they were hard to sell and getting a bit too old. Neither Phillip nor William had heard of this variety but were game to try them and they turned out well. They didn't yield as heavy as browns but heavier than the whites, They had a milder taste similar to the whites and the purple outer ring looked good on hamburgers and salads. Phillip took a quantity of the Spanish reds to the markets along with other surplus vegetables and he was amazed to find they were eagerly sought after, bringing premium prices so they agreed to order-in large quantities of seed for the following season. Locating sufficient seed was a problem until they got in touch with a seed distributor in France. The other item needed for the market garden was a ready supply of good quality well composted manure. Phillip already had a couple of places lined up and was searching around for more. They could always obtain plenty of artificial fertiliser, but who wants that when there are supplies of the real thing available. Quite a lot of farmers were changing over to much more intensive operations which did not need manure which they built up into large unsightly heaps and it was becoming a serious problem to dispose of. Phillip only had to find out who had the manure and arrange to collect it or better still have it delivered often free of charge. Sometimes he had to pay for the cartage but it was still very cheap. He mainly got pig and hen, and some cow manure.

The firm that supplied the onion seed sent a notice along with the seed describing new varieties of plants which they now had seed available for. The new seed was a close relative of sugar beet and beetroot. It was called Chard, a type of silver beet that came in three different colours, golden yellow, purple, and red. The leaves and stems were all edible and delicious but William was particularly interested in the stems. He reckoned they would work well in the Asian type stir-fries. Cut into short pieces and lightly fried they would be cheap, tasty and crunchy. The stems were so colourful as to lift the whole meal to exotic heights

They were mulching the tomatoes with a

mixture of straw and old well rotted manure which seemed to be doing nicely. When the mulch was seriously breaking down and covered in a white fungus mould after a few months, he thought it would probably grow mushrooms which he could use in his kitchen and were always hard to get and expensive. He believed that mushroom spawn could be planted in mid to late summer to get a crop of mushrooms beneath the straw in the autumn months. William caught up with Phillip one evening and suggested they go for a drive the following day. They had to use either Phillip's shooting brake or Vanessa's van, the main purpose of the trip was to visit mushroom growers to talk business and pick their brains. He had picked out three likely candidates and away they went. The first guy was keen to talk about possible supplies of mushrooms but otherwise not amenable to discuss how he produced them. They picked his brain and looked carefully at what they could see but he wasn't giving anything away. The second visit was to an elderly gent who could and did supply mushroom spawn and he was extremely helpful. The third visit seemed superfluous but the guy did help quite a bit, mainly with supplying the roadhouse with mushrooms direct instead of dealing through wholesalers. A deal was arranged to that end, thus rounding off a good day. Phillip was certain that he had gained enough information to grow a crop of mushrooms, although one thing they had learned today is that mushrooms can be the damnedest things to grow, even when you think you have all the answers.

William was now approaching his seventeenth birthday and he was looking forward to purchasing a nice vehicle and obtaining a licence to drive it. Both Phillip and Vanessa encouraged him to drive their vehicles whenever possible. They both agreed that William was a very competent driver even as good as if not better than either one of them. He had, of course been driving around farms virtually all his life. On his seventeenth birthday Vanessa drove William to the police station where the sergeant of police took him for a tour of the town streets and gave him his driver's license. He had never even held a learner's permit up to now so he was delighted. Being able to drive would make a huge difference to the way the outfit worked. It was so inconvenient having to rely on Vanessa or Phillip especially when the tractor was needed to take and collect materials for the market garden.

Of course the next problem was to obtain the most suitable vehicle not only for his personal use but also for business needs. William wanted to purchase a second hand vehicle mainly for his own use although he had plenty of money available to buy a new one. On the other hand Vanessa was pushing him to buy a new vehicle more with the business in mind than just private use. She pointed out that at the moment, until he finished studying at least he had little or no time for private motoring. The car yard in Chesterham was an Austin dealership. She steered William away from the private car section into the commercial show room to look at a vehicle called, 'Austin Omnivan'. These vehicles were built as general service vehicles and came in a number of formats. She introduced William to the sales manager and he took over the inquisition. He pointed out that these particular vehicles [Omnivans] were very versatile. If William opted to buy it as a work van he could save paying the sales tax then he would be restricted to 30 mph. However, he could purchase it as a private vehicle and pay the sales tax. He pointed out that the rear side panels were not part of the main vehicle because they were set in extruded rubber seals. This meant they could easily be removed and replaced with glass windows. Basically they were three seaters across the front. The 4 speed gear lever was mounted on the steering column thus allowing more floor and more seating space, but the dealer could supply and fit a two person seat on the driver's side behind the front bench seat, and still allowing access to the rear of the van through the sliding door on the passenger side. Eventually they bought the five seater window van, and agreed to pay the sales tax. Even so this was a very reasonable deal giving William so much variation and the dealer agreed to fit a towing bar to cart any objectionable materials behind. Once a suitable colour scheme and all the optional extras sorted Vanessa took her cheque book out of her hand bag and wrote out a cheque for the full amount. William quickly jumped in and objected strongly. This was to be his own van not the firms. Vanessa pointed out that there were all sorts of advantages in having the business own the van. There were huge tax savings initially and over the life of the van. The road tax and insurance were much cheaper and they were tax deductible against future business profits. William was not consoled although Vanessa's story seemed to make sense. Having agreed to suitable delivery date the deal was finalised. When William and Vanessa arrived back at the farm they settled in to have their first ever row. He had stewed over the ownership of the van all the way home. Vanessa was very apologetic for her bully girl tactics, which had surprised and devastated William. It took away all the pleasure of what had started out to be a very special day for him. He could see Vanessa's point of view but felt it should have been sorted out before visiting the car dealership. Better to grudgingly accept the van and make the best of it but it still rankled. To spend a large amount of money on anything he would need Vanessa's signature on the bank account. Maybe it was time to grow up and move on. He no longer needed to have a trustee bank account so he made an appointment to see the bank manager and change that. William was going to take quite a while to recover from this day's work but he had businesses to run and he still needed to spend much time with Michael. The next morning he returned to Michaels shop to work on a new body of beef. The smaller pork and mutton carcasses he was already happy with his knowledge and ability, but the much larger beef bodies were not so simple. There were so many different ways to break up the body into major sections and then so many more options to turn them into individual cuts because the customers had different needs to suit their menus and recipes. Michael greeted him warmly as usual and introduced the subject of buying the van and while he was sympathetic with Billy he thought that he should just accept the way things were. However he agreed to change the bank account now that there were no reasons to have restrictions on it. Vanessa did not share Michael's view on that but this time she had been trumped and reluctantly signed the papers. She was terrified that now William was free he might move on. She was going to have to treat him very circumspectly from now on.

Chapter Twenty One

William settled down with his knives, cleaver and meat saw to attack the carcass of beef. The beef arrived in two halves, already having been cut in half at the abattoirs where they had a big electric band saw to run down the backbone.

He discussed with Michael which was the best way they would need to break it down to suit the possible day's requirements. It was never going to be any more than a guess so they cut it up into the larger sections, which were then hung on the rail in the shop to be further cut up, de-boned and filleted to the customer's requirements, once they began to arrive with specific orders. Michael had now resorted to shortening William's name to Will rather than use his full handle but only in the workroom. Inevitably of course Michael soon became Mike. William was spending quite a lot of his days serving Mike's customers at the front counter, and the rest of his day in the rear of the shop helping and working with Ian, Mike's apprentice. Ian was mainly concentrating on the small goods side of the business. He processed all the off cuts into sausages and salamis and other small goods. Mike allowed Ian a good deal of leeway and as a result he made Will's special sausages and rissole mixes as well as his own. He had a good taste sensation and was beginning to understand the various tastes of herbs and spices. He and Will experimented with various flavours to spice up Wills stews and curries and they were getting some great results

One morning, Peter, the baker visited the butcher's shop and greeted William at the counter. After exchanges of pleasantries Peter remarked, "I heard you'd come down in the world William. I never expected you of all people to end up as a butcher boy. How much lower can you get?"

"My God Peter, you are a cheeky beggar. Haven't you heard the latest gossip around town? If I am ever to become a senior chef I need to understand some of the lower classes of food handling and preparation and I need to understand what makes them tick. I've just about finished here with Michael. I've picked his brain for many weeks and there is little more to be assimilated from that quarter, of course there was never much anyway, so next week I move on down the line towards the bottom of the heap. I had expected you to be au-fait with that knowledge, but not so, it seems. All being well at the cafe, I should be free to make an assault on next type of food business here in town."

Out of the corner of his eye William could see Michael standing in the adjoining doorway with a huge grin across his face waiting for Peter to walk into the deadly trap that William had set for him. Peter naively asked, "Oh that's great William, and who is the lucky participant in the next phase of your education?"

"Why Peter, don't you have any inkling of my next move? Starting very early on Monday next I will be waiting for your arrival at your premises ready to show you how to light your ovens and start baking our daily bread

Peter stepped back with a look of shock and horror on his face just as Michael and Ian split their sides with uncontrolled laughter. William on the other hand managed to keep a straight face saying, "I expected that announcement to shock you Peter but it is quite true. I need to know how you manage to stuff up so much bread every day, so into the lion's den I'll descend."

Poor Peter, took a little while to let all that bull settle into his brain then he too burst out laughing, grabbed William's hand and shook it vigorously, saying, "Well, well, so that's the way the wind blows is it and your very welcome I'm sure. You'd better come prepared for some serious hard work though. There'll be no doodling about at my place. Be prepared to lose a lot of sweat next week mate."

"True enough I believe the ovens do make your work area almost untenable since you can't afford to improve the air conditioning or buy a good fan."

Peter turned to Michael saying, "Oh dear me Michael is he like this all the time. Does this go on all day?"

Michael answered, "Yea mate and sometimes

it gets worse, Never mind Peter a few hours every day kneading and rolling dough around your place will quieten him down a bit and you might even make a man of him. We were hoping to tame him down a little bit but he just got worse so look out. We've been trying to work out how poor Vanessa copes with all his bullshit, she must be immune by now. He was bad enough before but now he has his driving licence and that bloody Austin van there's no stopping him.

"Don't let's blame poor Vanessa. Don't forget she is the female of the species therefore probably immune to all his crap. It's only the male to male scenario, like stags fighting to the death. Big horn rams and even elephants do it. They refer to it as testosterone. It's the male hormone sex driver. My God even roosters do it. Maybe if we completely ignore him he might attack someone else and leave us alone." Replied Peter.

"Hell yes, that might work, but it would be a dull old world without some of it. Hey! I've got it. The bugger needs a hot little lady in his life. That might slow him down a bit. Have you got someone in your mob who could help with that. Actually, now I come to think of it, the problem might even have fixed it's self. I noticed that cute little chick who works with him at the roadhouse, travelling around with him in his van a couple of times lately. If that comes to fruition we just might get some relief." Said Michael

"Oh heck, you must mean Melissa, she's from out of town somewhere. She did a bit of a training course with him at the café but I think she knew more about it than he did so he gave her a permanent job. Her Granny used to be one of the best pastry cooks in the county but she lives a fair way off. I bet that's where he'll go next because there isn't a decent pastry cook this side of Birmingham. If he manages to learn only half of what Elizabeth knows about that job he'll pass any test with flying colours." Replied Peter

"Yea your right about all that because Fred and Alison Jones, her parents, are really grand people. I bet they'd be thrilled to have William as their only son-in-law 'cause she's an only child, you know? That might be a win, win situation for all of us. Let's just hope he still has plenty cheek left in him anyway. He certainly brightens my day when he comes around to our shop, and you might be right about the female thing 'cause my missus thinks the sun shines from his arse."

"My God Michael, are you trying to tell me that it doesn't.

William, amazingly enough, saw very little of each individual member of the kitchen crew because of his split shifts, college studies, and trade training with Michael and Peter. However he was very aware of Melissa. She was filling out into a very beautiful young lady with a great sense of humour. She was always punctual, polite and hard working. Her smiles would almost dissolve Williams resolve never to become involved with any member of his staff. Just a fleeting smile as she said good morning, or good afternoon as the case may be, turned William's innards into a maelstrom. It often took them a while to cease churning around and settle back to somewhere near normal.

One morning she entered the kitchen as he was leaving and they crashed into each other. Melissa was busily apologising for daydreaming when she realised that William was not upset or even concerned. In fact he was looking quite delighted by the experience and who could blame him. It was not often that he had the pleasure of bumping into a lovely girl like Melissa. He put his arm around her waist to steady her lest she overbalanced. He was about to apologise for manhandling her when she said," "Gosh William, that was a lovely surprise. What a great way to begin the long hard day, don't you think?"

William retorted solicitously, "Melissa is that true, are you finding the work too hard or the days too long for you?"

She replied, "No of course not, I love working here, we all do. Hey, I heard you bought a new Austin van. Do you like it? Is it nice to drive?"

"The new van goes like a dream once you've mastered the column gear shifter. I had never driven a column change and it's a four-speed gearbox. I've hardly been anywhere in it yet, but over the next few weeks I should be able to get used to it. All I need now is a gorgeous young lady to fill the front seat beside me. Have you ever driven a column change Melissa?"

"Gosh, no. I've never even seen one let alone driven one. I understand that the new fords have some models like the Consuls and Zephyrs with it."

"I say, Melissa, you aren't working tomorrow during the day and I can arrange some time off. Do you feel like going for a spin in the country? I could pick you up at your place and we can enjoy a nice tea somewhere. Maybe, a nice little teashop, or a wayside café? What do you say?" Melissa blushed madly and replied, without any hesitation "Oh yes William that would be lovely. What time would you be able to call and pick me up?"

"Generally afternoons are the easiest for me so how about 1 o'clock at your home. I have your address of course." By this time they were both blushing bright red and smiling at each other. When William arrived home he told Vanessa about the trip. Vanessa replied, "Congratulations mate that should be lovely, a nice drive out into the countryside to get the feel of the Austin, even though you're still running it in and you won't find a nicer girl than

Melissa to accompany you. Well done, and good luck it's about time you enjoyed a bit of social life. The weather is quite settled at the moment so you should have a lovely drive in the countryside.

When William arrived at Melissa's home she was ready, and waiting. Hardly had he stopped than she ran out and jumped in beside him He had expected her mother to appear and lecture him how to behave but he spotted her peeping out through the lounge room curtains as they drove off.

William had never been involved with a girl in a social, or worse, romantic sense. He managed quite well at the roadhouse there he cut his teeth on older and often married women. He knew his ground there but out here was different. He was terrified of saying or doing the wrong thing or of even saying anything. To break the ice, he opened with, "I noticed your mother peeping out through the sitting room curtains keeping a close eye on her little chick"

She replied, "Oh yes, that's my Mum, tending her baby chicken like a clucky old hen. She promised she wouldn't do that, once I made it very plain that she was not to come outside and see me off. This is the first time I've ever been out on a date with a boy. She promised she wouldn't embarrass us. As you know I am an only child and she has met you quite a few times. So William, where are you taking me today? "

"I have decided to leave that up to you Melissa. I'm a complete stranger around here, whereas, you have lived around the place all your life so I assume you know all the nice places to go. I would love to see some of the cute little villages and scenery. With the river meandering close by there must be many nice spots to visit. Do you know of an extra nice tearoom or café where we could work our way round towards without you getting us lost."

"As this is my very first date I haven't done the romantic business yet although Dad often drove us around on Sunday afternoons. We usually picked up my Granny to get her out a bit. She gets a bit lonely at times now that Grandad isn't around anymore. I do know a few beautiful villages and a tearoom or two so turn left at the next cross roads and let's get to it." She replied.

"So you think this is a date, do you? Wherever did you get that idea Melissa? I thought you knew that I don't do dates. I never have. Although, I suppose I could give it a try if you can handle your end of the equation. Do I have to hold your hand and all that twaddle as well."

"You, young man, had better be kidding me unless you need a black eye. I have a massive left hook you know. Melissa had opted to sit in the middle of the long bench seat to be near William and she waved her sexy little fist in his face."

They were approaching a small picnic spot on the banks of the river Avon so William pulled into the tiny parking area and switched off the engine. He quickly turned to Melissa, threw his arms around her and gave her a big kiss on the lips. A first for both of them, as it turned out, and all the nicer for that. She sat back a little stunned, then broke out in a giggle, as the beetroot colour rose up from her neck and coloured her whole face. "What the heck was that all about? Is that part of the twaddle that you mentioned" She asked him.

"Very simply my girl, it was the only way I

could think of to shut you up, and it worked for a while. I'm going to do it again now, because I liked it, even though you apparently did not."

Melissa retorted, "Why don't you get on with it then I'll find out if it works for me? You cheated last time and caught me unawares. My lips were ready but my brain is a bit slow as you know." And of course they did do it again, long and sweetly and tenderly. William thought, if this is heaven, bring it on.

William would have been tongue tied all day in normal situations, but his smart arsed, kidding, and banter was something he practiced regularly on everyone around him and it relieved his shyness and embarrassment. His recent sessions with Michael and Peter had set him up for this moment and he was loving it. It meant that he did not have to think of soppy, romantic things to say because Mel was used to the banter and was not offended by it.

"Melissa then surprised William by saying, "You know what? From now on I'm going to revert to using your old name because it is so much softer and sexier than 'The Formal

William'. From now on I will only call you Billy, like I used to do, so get used to it."

"I have to agree with you there, Mel, I hated being William but it got me safely through a very sticky situation. Michael and Peter decided to call me Will inside their work areas, which is great but like you I loved being 'Billy the Kid'.

After a few more exotic kisses, and a good snog. Billy started the engine again as Melissa snuggled against him, making herself comfortable. He zigzagged around the scenic roads and quaint villages until it was time to find a tearoom with a view. Melissa guided Billy through a few more villages before asking him to stop near what could only be called a babbling brook near the edge of a cute village green with an assortment of mature trees surrounding it.

He spotted a small inconspicuous sign announcing 'Tearooms within'. A speciality was Devonshire teas and other goodies. Billy lead Melissa through the ornamental front door causing a small bell to tinkle somewhere within. They approached the counter as a middle aged lady appeared from out of the kitchen.

"Now then you young people can I get you a very nice meal or are you only after a snack." She asked.

We are quite hungry, so can you organise a large plate of mixed sandwiches, a scone or two with strawberry jam and cream and an assortment of cream cakes. And of course, a very large pot of tea to wash it down." Billy announced.

The lady suggested, "Seeing as it's such a lovely afternoon would you like me to serve you out on the lawn beneath the weeping willow tree or would you prefer to eat inside." Billy looked around the dining area and checked with Melissa who stated, "Oh, Outside for me thank you, we spend all our days eating in a café at work so outside would be a lovely change." After their meal had been served, the lady stopped for a chat. She was amazed to learn who they were and where they worked. She admitted that she and a couple of friends had actually visited the roadhouse on occasions. Monday and Tuesdays were a bit slow in the village she told them. Saturdays and Sundays were her busiest times because of the fishermen and their families along the river. So early in the week they sometimes went out for a drive and took tea along the way. She said the roadhouse absolutely amazed her and her friends. They normally avoided such establishments opting more for the country café but one day they were in need of petrol so decided to grab a quick cuppa at the same time. The décor really set them back a bit especially the new alfresco dining area. The menus and huge variety of foods available stunned her. They decided on a stir-fry meal and were delighted with the outcome and now they often call there. Instead of trying to cook for herself alone the lady said it was so refreshing to be waited on for a change and further more the prices were reasonable enough to enjoy quite frequently. Both ladies were keen to have a good Indian style curry. They both liked it hot and spicy and that's what they got. Eventually she left them alone to enjoy their meal before the tea got cold.

It was only a short drive to Melissa's home and they'd had a wonderful afternoon and vowed to do it again soon. Billy gave Melissa a great big kiss and cuddle as she got out and he walked her to the front door.

Chapter Twenty Two

Back on the job the following day William checked with Gregory Watson concerning his practicable abilities and next step forward. Finding a willing pastry cook was proving to be a serious problem. William studied every bit of written material about the artistry behind the noble art of pastry cooking and useful though it all was he needed lots of practical experience. Eventually he approached Vanessa with his problem and although relations had not been good between them since the Austin Saga, he thought she might know someone in the business, who could assist at least with some basic recipes to get him started.

Vanessa admitted that she had some basic skills and that she would help when and where she could. He then remembered her prowess at baking the best scones that he had ever tasted.

That would be a good start and of course her sponge cakes were legendary. She always cleaned up at the local agricultural shows. She had a shelf full of trophies that she'd won, around the district, not only the local shows but also the county show. Boy could this lady cook sponge cakes of every type imaginable.

In talking to Vanessa about baking and decorating cakes she half mentioned a familiar name without clarifying the details surrounding it. Billy solved the mystery of the familiar name when he next took Melissa out in the Austin. As they were driving along the quiet country lanes Billy mentioned his problems finding suitable tutors for various endeavours. A huge grin appeared across her face as she said, "Would it help if you could meet someone who is the greatest cake decorator that the county has ever known and she can bake, and does, bake the meanest cakes and pastries as well."

"I would promise to love you forever if that were possible." Billy said.

"Ok, you're on young man. Let's get started. Pull over into the next lay-by and kiss me properly this time." Melissa was in fact one week older than Billy so he took the quip in good part. After a nice necking session she said," Right you are turn right at the next intersection for about a mile then turn right again at the tee road. Billy new Melissa was leading him up the garden path. He had been along this road a number of times and knew there were no bakeries along the whole length of it. Furthermore there were no significant turn offs or commercial buildings either. What on earth was this girl up to? Was this to be payment for that glorious necking session or was there more to it? She told him to turn to the left besides a little stream and follow the cart track for a while until a large country cottage came into view. She ordered him to enter the driveway and stop near the front fence. She exhorted him to hurry up and get out of the van and follow her indoors. It was only when an elderly lady opened the door to them that the penny dropped. He knew this lady. He had entertained her at the café a time or two. My goodness, me, Melissa's Granny. Now everything made sense. Billy thought he was teaching Melissa to cook, but in fact, she was teaching him without his being aware of it.

Of all the cunning little minxes. He would make her pay for this day's work.

"Welcome to my humble home young man. To what do I owe the pleasure? My lovely granddaughter here doesn't normally come to visit me during the week. I've been told that you're to blame for that young man, is that true?" Elizabeth asked Billy.

"Guilty as charged Ma'am. Yes it's quite true I have been monopolising her spare time as I try to keep her out of trouble, but it's not easy. Maybe from now on I can probably rectify that somewhat if you are agreeable and well enough to help me out. You see I have a big problem at work. I need to upgrade my qualifications to become a qualified chef. I've been working with our butcher and baker but I couldn't locate a good pastry cook. I have tried to bake scones and sponges with only limited success although Vanessa reckons she can fix that problem given time. When I explained my needs to Melissa she assured me that she had exclusive access to the best pastry cook in the county and also the best cake decorator. Apparently this paragon is also the best baker of cakes and pastries, so here I am, at your mercy. I know it's a serious imposition expecting you to give up some of your valuable time on my behalf. I thought I might be able to get my time here to coincide with Melissa's days off so that I can drag her along with me to visit you and kill two birds with one stone, as they say. On the other hand, if you are spending most of your days knitting and bored out of your brain, and heaven forbid; watching daytime soapies on the television, this might be just what you need to re-enervate your lifestyle."

Granny Elizabeth produced a massive smile across her lovely face, threw her arms around Billy and kissed him firmly on the cheek. As she stepped back she took a good look into Billy handsome face and said with a grin, "Maybe I won't need Melissa any more, not if I have you for company Billy-Boy. I might even allow you to escort me out into the country in your Austin van.

Melissa shouted out, "Hey, you there Granny Elizabeth, you keep your hands off my fella. He's all mine. You can assist him from time to time but keep your grubby hands off. The banter and fun went on for a while but Billy managed to get some commitments from Elizabeth and agreed to suitable times and days. Tea and cake was the order of the day and William in his official capacity as chef suggested that he could improve Granny's income by purchasing any surplus cakes that they produced and the café would provide all the ingredients necessary. William was certainly looking forward to next week or two. He had a list of ingredients ready to take with him. He realised that it would be difficult to take Melissa with him each and every time but he would take her if it was at all possible for his own sake as well as for hers and her Granny's. They discussed using the ovens in the café but were aware that the dear old lady would prefer her own oven that she was used to and there would be no interruptions from other staff members. If someone suddenly opened an oven door it would be calamitous. William decided that, when he was ready to bake solo he would use the ovens at the farm not the café ones. The farmhouse was equipped with the slow combustion stove which would take a lot of practice to master but there was also a very large gas oven as well.

After Billy and Granny had worked together for some weeks she asked him, "We have covered quite a lot of my favourite recipes, quite successfully I might add so, today I wondered if there were any special treats that you might want to present to your customers. Maybe not on the everyday menu, but for special occasions such as birthday parties and such like, what do you say?"

"I hoped you might suggest something like that because I have one or two ideas hidden in my little brain that we could pursue. We always have plenty of eggs and vegetables on hand, might we put them together along with a nice fresh salad on special days. Of course I am thinking of a quiche or two. I am sure there are one or two tricks to assure me that they will always turn out special."

As per usual, Granny came up to the mark. Her first remark was, "Are you familiar with term, blind baking. You would need to master that first to prevent the liquids swamping the bottom pastry crust."

"Aha yes, up to a point, but a little coaching might be in order. I understand that the best way is to put a decent quantity of dried peas or some such heavy filling into the open pie crust after piercing the bottom with a fork, and bake that in the oven until the crust is well set. Are there any rules to determine the exact length of time required or is it just a bit of trial and error?"

Granny retorted with, "The word 'Error' must never come into the equation young man. We make sure that we get it right first time although it is not too critical, so get out the bowls and make a nice pastry like I've shown you while I get on with my knitting."

Billy did just that and when it was ready he rolled it out and pressed it into the shallow dish before piercing the base with a fork. Then Granny took over added a suitable quantity of dried peas set the oven temperature carefully and set the timer. That was all there was to it, simple.

Billy was already beating eggs and then he chopped up a quantity of smoked bacon before preparing the vegetables to be included. There were no set rules for the mixture it seemed, but a good balanced mixture of flavours and tastes was essential along with a selection of in-season herbs and various spices to taste. A good dressing of nutmeg on the top was always a bonus. This exercise had not used up too much time so Granny asked, "I assume there are many more to come Billy, am I correct?"

"Oh yes, you won't get off that easily Gran. The next item on the menu is sweets, namely cheese cakes. They are all special but I understand that some of them are easy no bake affairs, whilst others are called baked cheese cakes. Which are the best, and why."

Depending on the time available I suggest a no bake for a quick treat. Whereas, if time allows, the baked ones can be very exotic. For the no-bake ones a lovely, tasty, base mixture can be made using granita biscuits. There are a good many variations of this so get out your books and read it up when you get home. With the baked ones the same applies. The ingredients are long and varied so you can take your pick just make sure you get a good tasty balance of textures and flavours. Don't neglect the topping. I make up a tasty one with apricot nectar and a drop of rum. Whenever you have time to spare make up a series of each using different ingredients and toppings then decide which is best for you. You have the advantage that you can make up four or five at once and sell the surplus in the café.

Ok young man, that is more than enough for today so buzz off and do some homework. Next time you come bring the best of both kinds with you for us to taste together and make sure you bring my little girl to see me as well, I miss her terribly you know."

"Your every wish is my command 'oh mistress'. It shall be done, I promise. Billy's final remark brought a giggle from the old lady. She sent him off with a great big hug and cuddle followed by a lovely kiss on his cheek.

The following week Billy collected Melissa and headed out of town. In the rear of the van, carefully packed in strong cardboard boxes, there were three magnificent cheese cakes. Even Melissa had not been allowed to see these culinary masterpieces. Billy was so proud by the look of them, but would they be tasty, or even edible at all. He had not wanted to cut into them for a taste test until Granny Elizabeth had seen them in all their glory. He entered Granny's house carrying the no-bake cheese cake. It really looked great and Billy had carefully decorated the top with cream and other goodies. He stepped back and handed his big flat knife to Granny and held his breathe. Melissa was speechless. She had never seen a cheese cake the likes of this one. She collected three plates from the kitchen cupboard and three cake knives so as to receive a slice each. Wow, this really looked a treat. The taste test went well and Granny smiled a little before saying, "Well done young man but we still have a long way to go. What happened to the cheese cake that I asked you to 'bake' for me?" Billy went back out to the car taking Melissa with him. He picked up one box and gave it to Melissa to carry inside, then, picked up the other one and they strutted into the house with much pomp and ceremony. They placed the boxes onto the dining table and Billy opened his. Whilst the ladies were perving over that one he opened up the other box too. Amidst a good many oohs and aahs and the occasional, Oh my goodness me we can never cut into these cakes and destroy all your lovely work

William. Never-the-less, Granny picked up the knife again and cut three pieces from each cake. They were deathly silent as they tasted and retasted both samples then Melissa yelled out "Billy my love you've done it. They are both truly magnificent. They look fantastic and taste even better, don't they Gran? Don't you dare say they are not or we will never come to see you, not ever again."

"There you have it young man, the verdict loud and clear. I don't believe I can think of anything to add to that. Absolutely smashing. Well done I'm proud of you, come here and never mind Melissa." Billy approached her and Gran threw her arms around him, suddenly landing a smashing great kiss on his lips and a hug that almost strangled him. Once he recovered he said, "That was far better than any cheese cake I or anybody else could ever bake, Gran. I have a very delicate and special assignment for you now though. Gran, take your Granddaughter, here, in hand, and keep her with you until she can deliver a kiss even half as good as that."

Billy was far too slow to recover and copped

a whopping great punch on his arm from Melissa for his cheek.

They carefully repacked the remains of the cheese cakes to take back to the café with them because Granny had no hope of doing justice to them. William returned to Granny Elizabeth's house the following week because she had promised to teach him some of the finer arts of baking individual tarts and cup cakes. The most important snippet of information about baking individual tarts came early in the piece. These little beauties need to stay firm enough to be picked up and handled as they are fed into hungry mouths. There is nothing more soul destroying than sitting in a posh restaurant in one of your finest outfits, with all your posh friends watching on, as the delightful fruit tart breaks up before your eyes and slides down your beautiful blouse or gown. Once the tart shells had been blind baked, Granny poured a spoon full of melted cooking chocolate into the base of each one and allowed it to spread out evenly across the bottom and set firmly before adding any of the ready prepared fillings. She stated the obvious, "Once the chocolate has set, it moisture proofs and strengthens the pastry shell which prevents most of the embarrassing collapses and mess.

Chapter Twenty Three

Meanwhile, back at the market garden, Phillip and his workers were doing a fantastic job. Most of the crops had grown and yielded well and they were proving very profitable. The green house crops, mainly tomatoes had excelled all expectations. Most had been either used in the café or sold directly out at the front counter. Quite a lot had been gobbled up by Ernie and sold in his green grocery store. He was delighted with the quality and size. William had used up much of the lower grade fruit to make up tomato relish, tomato chutney, tomato soup, and tomato sauce. Thus only the very best were marketed in the two shops often at premium prices. Once again this year he harvested all the unfinished green tomatoes and made large quantities of green tomatoes relish and chutney to be used in his kitchen or sold over the front counter. The garden and fields were looking pretty drab by now as all the summer vegetables had been harvested. The remainder were Brussels sprouts, winter cabbages and root crops. Phillip and company were cleaning up the crop residues and had begun ploughing up any ground that was cleared of crops and no longer needed. How long would their good luck hold or would it suddenly end soon? This had all been too fortunate to continue indefinitely. It was early autumn when disaster struck. The weather decided to spoil the party. One morning William awoke to heavy rain. He was not too worried as it was that time of the year and the soil needed a good steady soak to fill up the subsoil for next year's crops. Most of the plants likely to be damaged by too much rain had already been harvested. The root crops could stand plenty of water but the rain did not stop, it continued to rain for a whole week. Up in the nearby hills it rained day and night resulting in a savage rise in the river level. Phillip and William studied the situation one morning then decided to try and save as much of the root crop as they could before they were inundated by the inevitable flood. They called in all their usual, and reserve workers to get stuck in and harvest carrots, parsnips, leeks, celery, potatoes and Swedes. Most of the work had to be handled in the old fashioned way, by hand, because the ground was far too wet for the tractor, even before the flood waters inundated it. Many of their neighbours shook their heads in amazement to see all these workers slopping about in their Wellington boots covered in mud. It looked like an Asian paddy field for growing rice. "What sort of idiots are you? Get out of there and leave it alone until it dries out. You're only making a great, big, puggy mess," they said as they stood back shaking their heads.

Every day the river rose to new heights and began to spread out onto the fields. William told Phillip to be very careful for the safety of the workers. He claimed that it was better to lose some of the crop rather than risk the lives of their staff.

The wettest areas were harvested first ahead of the flood then they worked their way up onto higher ground. They laid sandbags in the greenhouse doorways so they should be safe. William and some of the crew worked all through the night carting the produce that had been saved, into the barns, spreading it out to dry off a bit before storing it in heaps and bins. By the time the water inundated the rest of the field only the poor old sprouts and winter cabbages were left to take potluck alongside a small area of Swedes. By then the rain had finally stopped but there was a huge amount of water left up in the hills ready to pour down into the river which continued to rise to never before seen heights. Finally the river levels began to fall, slowly but surely. Absolutely worn out with little or no sleep for days on end William and Phillip bogged their way out around the edges of the fields to assess the damage. There was still a lot of water on the ground but it was static and would soak in given time. They had lost a certain amount of topsoil in some areas but had actually gained some in others.

They were fortunate that the garden and the fields were situated on a higher piece of the river bank although not much higher than most of the surrounding areas and therefore their losses were not significant. Balancing that were the market prices. Many of the farms and market gardens throughout a large area were inundated for many weeks and what remained of the crops had rotted in the ground. This of course meant that any crops like theirs that had actually been saved were fetching record prices. The homestead and greenhouses were fine as was much of the land. Winter ploughing was going to be held up but there was still plenty of time. Once the water subsided Phillip checked out the winter greens and although battered they would harvest well he thought, They would slot into a heavily depleted market and as a result prices were extremely favourable. Their Brussels sprouts, Savoy cabbages and the January king cabbages had benefited from the rains. The heads were very large and very solid. They brought record prices at the local markets. Many of them were shipped off to the big city hotels and restaurants to help fill the shortages there.

One thing William could be sure of was

that life was never ever going to be boring. The market garden project in all of its facets was constantly changing almost daily in fact. Without Phillip's, input and high endeavours, very little of it would have worked at all let alone become an unqualified success. Most of the work force revered Phillip. He was a caring and considerate employer with heaps of skills and more importantly ingenuity. Being one step ahead of the game was so important and Phillip seemed to have a knack to foresee future possible problems as well as future potential benefits. He and William made a great team as they worked their way through problem after problem without crossing swords. Their agreeable natures were legendary throughout the business. William of course, had the café to run and like Phillip he had a great team along with him. One leading light was of course Melissa. She was a natural leader and those around her revered her natural skills both as a cook and as a manager. They had always had a great working relationship and now their social life had matured into a form of utopia. They often wrangled and wrestled, [verbally and physicallyl which helped to clear the air. Their developing relationship with Granny Elizabeth was often a great stress breaker and it defused the odd situation before it could become serious. Amazingly, William had not had much involvement with Fred and Alison, Melissa's Parents, although they got on well together. They didn't avoid each other and it was mainly their shift work that interfered with their relationship. William was a bit concerned that Fred would feel that he was stealing his little girl, but in fact he seemed to relish the idea. After all, William had helped to train Melissa and set her on the right path to a great career as a cook and a manager. One afternoon Melissa suggested that they all get together for a family dinner party at her home. Melissa owned a Morris minor 1000 sedan by then so she volunteered to collect her Granny and deliver her safe to her own parent's home. William offered to supply the sweets course, which was happily accepted by Alison, leaving her free prepare and cook the main meal, a roast loin of pork organised by Michael, Vegies from the market garden, and herbs from Fred's garden as well as Alison's skill with her oven.

Fred and Billy made themselves comfortable in the lounge for a good old natter about sport and weather and life in general. After a while, Nan excused herself from the kitchen and asked permission to join the men, which they gladly accepted and they were glad to change the subjects. They were all interested in gardening especially vegetable growing and the impact of the disastrous floods. Fred was quite surprised at how well Phillip and Billy had coped with the bogs. His garden was quite high above any floodwaters but, as he said, the ground was totally saturated with the rainfall, anyway, and didn't need a flood as well. As expected their meal was quite a triumph. After all, how could three cooks possibly get it wrong. Just let's forget the old adage about too many cooks, three [our three] definitely were not too much. William's sweets were well accepted although they were all pretty full after the dinner so they were delayed for supper snacks instead. To save Melissa driving at night William bade them all goodnight and opted to drive Nan home in the Austin. The evening was voted a complete success and everyone vowed to do it again soon.

A few days later Phillip called in to the roadhouse, partly to discuss another profitable market day and run a few ideas through William's brain. He had been thinking about mushrooms. Slapdash though it was, growing them beneath the tomato crop had yielded a goodly amount of mushrooms and Phillip was keen to continue in the future. He was quite surprised when William announced that he had been thinking along similar lines. Having seen a few growing sheds and talking to growers had set the roots of a plan. Among the farmyard buildings there were a number of stone built granaries and other similar barns and storage rooms that were no longer in use. William suggested that with a minimal amount of adaptation they might be ideal for growing mushrooms. False ceilings preferably insulated would be needed to help keep the temperature under control. Some type of cooling device and temperature control would be essential to get maximum growth from the crop. They would need to erect some sort of shelving throughout each buildings to grow the crop on, as well as a steady supply of straw and spores. A quantity of the new style polythene piping would be required for irrigation.

The men went for another tour of the countryside especially to see the elderly gent who had supplied them with the spores last year to see if they could commandeer more if not all of his output. The gentleman was more than willing to sell his whole output to one grower and he had quite a lot of redundant growing shelves that they were able to acquire for only a nominal fee. They were in business. Phillip was also quite happy to spend as much of his time as possible to learn the techniques and greatly increase the output to meet their requirements and reduce the old chaps workload substantially.

A local carpenter soon had one of the granaries ready to plant and was working on the others. A redundant refrigeration plant became available at scrap prices from a nearby abattoir, now defunct. They were going to need the services of a qualified electrician to rewire the buildings and rearrange the lighting. He needed to install a new substation to cope with the increased load and wire up the refrigeration unit. Whilst retrieving the unit from the abattoirs he was able to get quite a lot of ancillary equipment needed to go with it, thus saving a great deal of money because new electric switch boards were expensive.

One obvious requirement was a qualified plumber to pipe water supplies into the granaries and set up a drainage system to prevent any excess water from damaging the floors and shelves. The local plumber was a young forward thinking guy who was recently qualified and had studied the use of a new product called black polythene piping. This stuff was easy to use because it could easily be bent around corners without extra fittings. It was easy to cut to length and came with an assortment of fittings to join it together. It didn't need a blowlamp to heat it up and didn't need threading tools to make the joints. From their own previous mushroom growing enterprise Phillip gleaned a couple of serious staff members who had thoroughly enjoyed the experience and were keen to take it on full time. The knowledge and practical experience they had gained in past years set them up to lift this new endeavour to new heights. They were a very innovative pair, who were quite prepared to experiment in all the facets of the business. They were eager readers and scoured book and magazine shelves in the search for those snippets of information that can and do make a big difference to the outcome of any project. Until the buildings were ready to occupy, Phillip, took the two girls to a bed and breakfast house in the village near to the old man's sheds to work with him and pick his brains as well. The girls were ecstatic. They worked well together and enjoyed each other's company. The old chappie let them carry out most of the work whilst he explained the techniques needed to capture the moments. The girls couldn't wait to get home again and try all this out.

The gent took some spore from a refrigerator saying, "I stole this when I went to Holland. I just hope it's not poisonous. This is Dutch brown cap. Slightly stronger than our white one and a much nicer flavour all round so it should go well if we can get it to grow. They are experimenting with a few Japanese varieties but they were guarding it like gold. One was 'Oyster shell' which looked fabulous and a odd looking thing called 'Chittake', I think it was. Apparently in Japan they often dry the fungus and export it in small packets, which means they can have mushrooms all the year round. They re-hydrate quite well with only minimum loss of flavour, so they told me. If I was twenty years younger I would try freeze drying our field mushrooms or the Dutch browns. There would be a great demand for them out of season I'm sure. Maybe that's something you girls could play around with in your spare time. It can't be too hard if the Jap's. can do it successfully, why can't you? Have a go sometime? It won't hurt too much if you fail and could make a lot of money if it works out. We often throw away misshaped ones that are ok but don't look nice so it's no loss if it doesn't work. If you think it's a goer we can build a workable drier without too much trouble or cost. If we manage to pull it off we can get William to organise some plastic bags and a machine to seal them up like they do with a heap of stuff in the super markets. Once they were back at home the girls explained to William and Phillip about the drying procedure and they agreed to investigate the process, partly for their own use to get a continuous supply of mushrooms for the café kitchen and partly as a saleable product to hotels and restaurants. William made a phone call to the packaging company who had supplied the take-away cartons. He was transferred to a scientist on the team who was very keen to experiment with the packaging. William realised that there were quite a number of avenues to expand any business in the UK. In the late 1950's England was still recovering slowly from the privations and limitations of the second world war and many doors were opening up for anybody with enough guts to barge in and give it a go. A good many products had only recently been released from the rationing process especially fresh meat so a whole new world was only now opening up in all phases of trade and commerce. Even in agriculture, horticulture and market gardening there were new varieties of plants to experiment with, and experiment they did.

Apart from all the excitement at the roadhouse and the market garden William and Melissa were enjoying their togetherness. Alright, let's call it loving because that's what it was. They were deeply in love with one another and relishing the fact. There was never enough time to indulge their togetherness but they took every chance they could to be together, often in the Austin van. They both had a great love of the countryside and an avid love affair with nature, especially the birds and other wild life. Billy had often roamed free around the fields, woods and streams surrounding the farm where he grew up but love was never mentioned or practiced in their household. Having someone like Melissa not only to soak up his love and adoration but also to love him back to distraction was unbelievable and very heartening. Oh, how a quick hug or cuddle and a kind word could have enhanced his young life and given him hope for the future. Loving Melissa had brought a new experience into Billy's life. He now had a family around him for the first time in his life.

Melissa's parents, Fred and Alison adored

Billy and welcomed him to their home. He often called in for a cuppa and a chat even when Melissa was working. Even a nice evening stroll around Fred's garden was a welcome therapy and gladdened his heart. Every visit culminated in a great big hug and a kiss on the cheek. On top of all those thrills there were the attentions of Granny Elizabeth. Prior to Billy's entry into her life she had been a happy but somewhat lonely old soul after the death of her husband. She always had plenty to occupy her time, both indoors and in the garden however living as far remote as she did she lacked human company. When Billy and Melissa were out and about they often called in to share time with the old lady and take her for long drives around the beautiful villages. An added bonus was a visit to Alison who was often on her own during the day when Fred was working. Billy, for the very first time in his life was utterly swamped with love and affection. It seemed like forever since that dreadful day of his Grandfather's funeral in Clifford village. The pain was still with him daily but these days it was slowly healing but would never be forgotten. He loved his Grandad dearly and his love was returned a thousand fold whenever they were together. Love is the great miracle of life and should be embraced at every opportunity and shared around with everyone. Love and knowledge are useless commodities unless they are shared, willingly with others.

Melissa and Billy, seldom indulged in any formal entertainment, it wasn't their style. However there was one exception, ballroom dancing. They both loved to dance and most weekends there would be a village hop somewhere around. It wasn't often they managed to get an evening off together but when they did they donned their glad rags and hopped in with great enthusiasm. They had a great time dancing jiving and cuddling each other to the sounds of lively dance music. Music was usually provided by local musicians and often went right through the night. It wasn't unusual for some of the dancers to return home and go straight out to work.

Neither Billy nor Melissa were interested in alcoholic beverages, sure they had both tried various types of alcoholic drinks but never found any one that appealed to them Fortunately the café didn't have a licence to sell or serve alcohol. Now that the alfresco dining area was up and running well there was some suggestions that the café should check out the licensing authority to allow them to serve alcohol supplied by the diners themselves but neither Billy nor Vanessa were influenced in any way. Because the dining room was available 24hrs per day it meant that staff were starting their shifts at all hours of the day and a close watch had to be kept to prevent staff arriving under the influence of alcohol and even worse surreptitiously drinking during their shift. One or two staff members had their job cancelled as a result of breaking the rules in this regard. Once Vanessa was satisfied that the alfresco dining hall was a complete success and would be profitable she obtained quotes to add concertina doors along the open side to enable it to be used all year round. She advertised for suitable trades people to offer different types of doors to get the best design for the area. At last a suitable arrangement of concertina doors was accepted and duly installed. It included some fixed panels and sliding glass doors, with a section of glass and wooden folding doors at both ends. She pushed the contractor hard intending to have it complete whilst the summery weather held. The final result was a vast improvement and was to be much enjoyed by all. The café was so busy now that it created a, much needed, dining experience and was to be well used for functions such as weddings, birthday celebrations, yes, and even funeral wakes. As you would realise this created a strong demand for capable staff to cook, serve and clear away. William's training deal with the college was paying off big time. A steady supply of young people was now available to him.

Chapter Twenty Four

Life had been extremely pleasant for Billy and Mel after all the drama of the floods and the massive cleanup that followed. Phillip was quite certain they had benefited greatly as a result of their immediate action to harvest the root crops. Most of the produce had been successfully harvested and the vastly inflated prices had more than made up for labour costs and any loss of quantity.

As winter slowly slipped into spring and the weather improved. Phillip and his team had sorted out the mess in the market garden and a new crop was showing great promise.

Although early days as yet the girls were confident that they could get the mushroom business off to a good start. They had persevered with the drying program and with some assistance from Phillip and William had designed what appeared to be a working dryer for the fungi. It still needed a good deal of tweaking and improving to become efficient, but it worked well enough for now.

Billy and Melissa were now very comfortable with their love for each other. Both of the young people were looking forward with great anticipation to the end of summer. They would both turn 18 years of age late August early September with only a few days between them. Billy and Fred were planning a fantastic celebration which meant a good deal of reorganisation to get the rosters in order so neither one of them would be working on the day and that plenty of the staff would be available to cope with the catering. Vanessa volunteered to handle all the rigmarole of the invitations, table places and décor etc. with some input from Alison and Elizabeth. However the big celebration almost never happened.

Late one Sunday afternoon a tourist coach pulled up out in front of the café. William asked Vanessa if, they had booked in before hand. Vanessa had no knowledge of the visit but, no matter, they could cope. Just a couple of quick phone calls to round up reserve staff and they were all set. William looked out at the coach and exclaimed in horror, "Oh my God Father this is all we need"

Vanessa rested her hand on Billy's arm and realised that he was shaking like mad. She asked, "What on earth is the matter? William why are you upset? There's only one coach and we often cope with two or three."

William whispered, "True enough Boss but look at the name on side. That bus belongs to Rodgers & Son's coach lines. I used to travel to primary school on one of their buses. The owner's son travelled on the same bus and we were both in the same class. The bus depot was situated in a nearby village and my Dad was friendly with the owner and their drivers. Let's just hope my old man hasn't decided to go for a tour through the West Country and Wales with them."

"I don't believe there could be any problems either way but we'll keep a careful eye on them, in fact, I'll put a call through to Sergeant Terence, it's about time he paid us another visit."

Once all the passengers had disembarked

the driver stepped down and oh my God, It was James Rodgers himself. He immediately recognised William and called out to him before William had time to disappear. William turned around saying, "Are you talking to me sir. Take a look at this badge." He then pointed out to the driver the name badge that he always wore at work, 'William Riley'. "Who were you expecting to see here today? I have never set eyes on you."

"By heck you look like a fellow I knew at school, sorry pal." The driver said. He turned around and walked outside calling out to someone as he went. "Hey there, Joe, put that stinking old pipe out and come here. There's a bloke in the café that's the spitting image of your Billy, but his names different"

Aye well our Billy changed his name, I think to Riley, Or summat like that. Let's be having a look at 'im. Where is the bugger?

"He appears to be the cook or chef or some such. He just went through that double door into the kitchen."

Come on then let's be 'avin' a look at 'im." Joe said as he pushed his way behind the counter and through the door into the kitchen. "Now then you rotten bugger, I've got you at last. Come 'ere you rotten sod. I'll put my belt over your arse. You caused the death of your mother. She drowned in yon quarry because of you, and our Maude has left home as well." He said as he pulled his big leather belt out of his trousers. Vanessa went berserk and grabbed his arm as he attempted to strike Billy and shouted at him to get out and leave Billy alone. Joe grabbed Billy's arm and pulled him around as he hit out with the belt. Vanessa was hanging on to his arm and took most of the sting out of the vicious blow. She was determined to protect her Billy from this thug.

The kitchen hands were only young girls and not much help, so it was only Billy and Vanessa, until the rear door suddenly burst open, at about the same time as the swinging doors out into the dining area also burst open. Sergeant Terence and two constables charged in through the rear door at the same time as Michael and Peter burst in through the swing doors. Joe put up a heck of a struggle before the police locked a pair of handcuffs on him and dragged him outside kicking and screaming all the way. They threw him into a police van and quietly left the scene heading for the police station Amazingly the whole scenario only lasted for a few seconds before all was quiet again.

Vanessa was crying her eyes out more in relief than anything else. She and Billy shared a massive hug, kissed cheeks and wiped away their tears. Turning around to the staff, Billy said, "We are so sorry you had to witness that disgusting display of anti-social behaviour. It's all over now and you can rest assured it will never occur again in my kitchen. Now, maybe you can see why we are so adamant that you do not ever get involved with alcohol. That man was completely out of control, and not really responsible for his actions. We are so glad that none of you got tangled up in that fracas. If anything like that ever does happen here or elsewhere just step back and move away. OK, teas are on the house, coffee if you'd rather, and thanks again. As soon as we clear this coach any of you that feel you want to go home it will be ok. We'll pay you your full allowance for the rest of your shift. I'm sure we'll manage for the rest of the night. Later on the police might want a quick word with you all but I very much doubt it. Both of the girls stayed on the job much to everyone's relief.

Some time later the Sergeant and one constable did come back to interview the bus driver. They told him they were not at all impressed with his actions and were considering arresting him on a charge of inciting a fracas, or even a riot. The driver was very badly shaken up by the whole affair and scared for his licence. He told the police that this was the first time he had had any problems and it would be the last. He was horrified at the violent outcome because he had known Joe for many years and he was surprised to see his reactions to what he thought would have been a happy reunion. Of course, James, the driver, didn't know much of the initial problems between Joe and Billy or of Ethel's death. He was able to assure the police that he was not part of any plot to attack Billy and neither he nor Joe had any idea that Billy worked in that café. The police let him off with a stern warning, mainly in deference to the waiting passengers.

Back at the police station Joe was still kicking up a riot. He finally calmed down sufficiently to explain that he only wanted to find out how their Billy had managed to get this far away from home without anyone spotting him or his crazy bike and trailer. He realised that his approach was ridiculous and was never going to be any help. The police Sergeant showed Joe a copy of the story of his escape from Yorkshire. He congratulated Billy on his ingenuity and fortitude, especially surrounding his injuries. He showed Joe a copy of the photographs that the police had taken of Billy's back and gave him a copy. The written report he took back and placed in the police file. He then stood up saying, "Joseph Charles O'Leary I am about to charge you with savage assault on your son William and hereby warn you that anything you say will be taken down and used in evidence against you at your trial, You can keep that copy of the photograph to remind you of your sins, shame on you. If you ever have the affront to show your ugly face anywhere near our town, and more importantly, near Billy, you will be arrested and tried for this day's efforts as well as the previous assaults on Billy. You can go now. Get away out of our town, in fact right out of our county altogether."

"How the bloody hell can I leave town, yon bus will have left by now?" Joe replied. The constable chipped in with, "It's a pity you never considered that before you kicked up a shindig here in our town. I'll take you out to where the overnight bus stops and if we are quick you might be able to catch tonight's bus as it is nearly due. Get outside quick and let's be rid of you. We don't want you hanging around here until tomorrow night's bus"

In the weeks prior to Melissa's birthday, Billy took her to the nearby towns where there were jeweller's shops. They looked at many different types of jewellery including bracelets, pendants, broaches and signet rings. If nothing else William was able to assess Mel's ring size and her preference for different styles of jewellery especially engagement and signet rings. He wanted to buy her something very special for her eighteen birthday. He finally settled on a fantastic locket and chain. He felt this would be more acceptable than a signet ring for working in the kitchen because she could wear it all the time when she was working. He located a special photograph of Melissa and a similar one of himself. He settled on images which would face each other when carefully installed. When the locket was open he faced her and she faced him. The following day Billy rang the jeweller and placed the locket 'on hold', promising to place a deposit the next morning. He called at the jeweller's the very next day to complete the transaction and further study the shop contents because he needed a wrist watch for himself.

Vanessa and Melissa's family went ahead with the preparations for Melissa's party. Her birthday happened to be on a Saturday, which was fortuitous. Mel knew they were preparing for a large celebration of some sort, but, as she was not likely to be on duty that weekend, she stayed away from the arrangements. Meanwhile she was aware that her Mum and Grandmother were cooking up a storm for some reason. She expected a small family get together on Saturday with William as guest of honour of course. Meantime, discreet arrangements were being made at the café to decorate the Alfresco area. A large barbeque stove had been installed in one corner with a hatchway through the wall into the kitchen. It had a wide canopy above the top and a flue with extractor fans through the roof. This cooking area could now be incorporated with the kitchen amenities to make life much easier for the staff. Melissa's party was to be the test flight for this new amenity.

William arranged for himself and Melissa to have the whole weekend free of work related commitments starting on Friday morning. During Friday they went off to a large shopping emporium to further examine assorted jewellery but nothing smacked them in the eye. On the Friday evening Billy drove them to a very upmarket hotel where the cuisine was second to none. They enjoyed a sumptuous dinner before entering the lusciously appointed ballroom for a special evening of ballroom dancing. Whilst Mel attended the ladies room Billy passed a notice to the Master of Ceremonies. During a break in the dancing, the M.C called for a little decorum because he had one or two announcements to make. Melissa's Eighteenth birthday was the last on the list. She was startled when he announced 'HER' name and details. Tears were rolling freely down her cheeks as she bestowed Billy with the biggest kisses and hugs that even put Granny Elizabeth's in the background

The dancing continued until very late then Billy drove her home for a massive necking session on her doorstep. Finally with one last kiss he wished her happy birthday, as it was already long after midnight. Saturday morning was going to be full on as all the preparations began to come together.

All the results of the big bake off were still at Granny Elizabeth's place, so that was where Billy headed first. Thank goodness Vanessa had encouraged him to buy the Austin because it was soon full to capacity with culinary delights. He wanted to collect them early just in case Melissa ventured over to see her Gran during the morning. He delivered them to the restaurant where a large group of employees and friends carefully set them out on the tables. There was a large three tiered birthday cake among them that William had crafted personally. All the decorations he had made by hand and assembled into a magnificent array, with some input from Granny Elizabeth. On the top layer there was a carefully sculpted figure of Melissa in a fantastic full length ball gown. There appeared to be some missing pieces around the statue but it was actually complete for now. The cake was carefully hidden from view until needed. Billy checked and rechecked that every little detail was in place ready for the star of the show. Then he rushed back to the farm for a nice hot shower before dressing in his finery. He was used to wearing a bow tie at work but full evening dress was something else.

Billy drove round to Melissa's home to collect her. Her father Fred was ready to leave in her little Morris car with Granny in the rear seat. Fred and Alison appeared with their arms full of presents which they placed in the boot of the Morris, then they were off, but where to? Melissa was completely in the dark as to what was about to eventuate. She was knocked for a six when she saw Billy's outfit and said, "It looks like it was a good idea to have a bath before I put my clean knickers on. You look a million dollars. I would give you a great big kiss except for my makeup. Where the heck are you taking me my love?"

"Hey it's Saturday night and we're on duty as you know, so it's off to work young lady. Don't think for one moment that you're getting the night off just because it's your birthday, madam."

"Are you trying to tell me that you are going to work in your penguin suit? I don't believe you for one minute," Billy.

"No of course not, silly, I'll take it off when we get to the café. I'm doing a special striptease for your birthday party. We couldn't afford a real party so this will have to suffice."

Billy stopped beside the doors into the alfresco dining area, jumped out and opened the passenger door for Melissa. Scooping her up in his arms he carried her into the waiting arms of her family, calling out "Happy Eighteenth Birthday Sweetheart." He then kissed her long and soundly to prove he meant it. There was a fantastic array of foods on the tables plus great aromas coming from the new barbeque. The ladies organised seating arrangements at the tables whilst the men collected all the presents from the boot and displayed them on a table on the stage. When most of the appetites were satiated someone called for the presents to be opened so Billy escorted Melissa onto the stage to do the honours with some assistance from Alison. They presented a magnificent display and Melissa was utterly nonplussed. She carefully perused the scene then realised that there was nothing with Billy's name on it. The look on her face told the sad story until Billy pushed the final package into her hands saying, "Happy birthday my love." It was only a small parcel, which she opened with great anticipation. She was half expecting some sort of jewellery but she was speechless at what she saw. It was of course the locket and chain. Melissa was so pleased she was battling to speak and the water works were stuffing up her makeup. Whilst all the ladies were oohing and aahing over the locket Billy gave the wait staff a pre-arranged signal. The waiters perambulated around the room supplying all the kids with glasses of lemonade and the adults with champagne flutes. The M.C. called the meeting to order before proposing a toast to the party girl. With three cheers ringing in their ears everyone joined in with "For She's a Jolly good fellow," as Billy showed her how to open the locket.

Melissa was clinging on to Billy and the tears were pouring down her face as she kissed and hugged him tightly. Billy noticed that Fred and Alison were about to escort Granny Elizabeth forward but he stopped them for now. Melissa was holding the locket carefully when she asked, "Is this really for me Billy? It must have cost a fortune, can you afford it?"

Billy replied quite loudly so most of the guests would be able to hear him. "Of course not sweetheart, I only borrowed it from the jeweller so we could impress everyone tonight. You can keep it until Monday then I must return it to the shop."

There was a stunned silence among the guests and Melissa's face crumpled in pain before Billy pulled her into his arms again saying loudly, "Of course it's yours to keep you silly girl. It's a sincere token of my love for you but it comes with a big snag as you suspected. You have to accept this as a further token of my love and agree to marry me soon." So saying, he held on to her left arm slipping the gorgeous ring that she had also admired on to her ring finger. Melissa shed many more tears then a thought struck her, as she asked him, "Were Mum, Dad and Granny Elizabeth in on this as well."

He replied with a big grin across his handsome face, "No of course not. This was strictly Men's business. I only talked it over with your Dad and he said if I didn't ask you tonight he would shoot me with his old double barrelled shotgun."

More lemonade and champagne was called for as the waiters rolled out a silver trolley with the elaborate cake on board. The top layer was now complete. Fred and Granny Elizabeth had added the rest of the statue, which was naturally, Billy's image. Together Billy and Melissa held onto Billy's own steak knife, borrowed from his kitchen, and they cut a big slice off the bottom layer before the other layers were removed. Billy realised that quite a few people were not fond of fruitcake so for the centre layer he had baked a beautiful cream filled sponge cake instead. Once the cake had been sliced and served the M.C. called for order and a bit of shush then said. "Thank you all for attending to night to help celebrate Melissa's eighteenth birthday. However, I got the feeling that we were all irrelevant. Billy could have managed quite well, on his own. Congratulations Melissa. What I was wondering is, who will be the star next weekend, because I am sure you're all aware that Billy also turns eighteen then, on the Fifth of September. Congratulations Billy. The assembled guests and staff went wild with congratulations, three cheers, and that famous song.

THE END

POST SCRIPT

Melissa's party went on most of the night and everyone was on the verge of collapse. No one had any idea, what, if anything was planned for the next weekend but it would probably be one great anticlimax after Melissa's shindig. The roadhouse and café surely could not afford another such party, much as everyone loved Billy, and would want to let him know how special they thought he was.

He was slowly coming to terms with the event concerning Joe O'Leary, and he was still expecting more repercussions from that event. He was dreading having to attend court to face his old man and give evidence against him. Also he was mortified at the thought of having to drag his lovely new friends and family into court to support him.

His life at the moment was running so smoothly and happily that he wanted nothing to spoil it, least of all, anything so unsavoury as the fight with his father. Sergeant Terrence and the local police force would do everything in their power to end the standoff. After all he was only a few days away from his eighteenth birthday and that should settle the matter once and for all.

Brian O'Donnell

352

Shake, Rattle and Roll

A 15 year old school boy is invited to become part of an exciting adventure extending over three summers in Yorkshire and Lancashire with touches of Durham and Northumberland thrown in along the way. Driving a steam driven, historical, agricultural tractor on iron wheels over vast distances each weekend to attend charity and historic rallies and _field days. Travelling over the Pennine Mountains and north Yorkshire moors to attend some of the greatest rallies and gala weekends ever experienced. He steered the tractor on some of the busiest roads in the north of England including many miles along the great north road now called the a1 highway, he guided his "charge" through many of the great industrial towns and cities of the north such as Leeds, Manchester, Newcastle, Durham and Chester-le-street.

Brian named his book "Shake Rattle and

Roll" due to the discomfort of driving an iron monster on iron wheels with cross strakes.

You've Got To Be Kidding

My book contains [56] very readable, short, fun, stories about the many humorous situations that life has placed me in over the years. I have tried to introduce some of the quirky characters that I have met in my daily life. there were many very humorous incidents and others more startling and ghostly in character. However, life has a habit of delivering shattering blows to people and I was no exception to that rule, as will become obvious to my readers. In spite of all this, I believe that I have been much more fortunate than many others around me. I sincerely hope that you enjoy reading my stories as much as I enjoyed writing them.

354